Happily Ever After
COOKBOOK

ORIGINAL RECIPES *for* BOOK LOVERS

CONTENTS

APPETIZERS & SIDES

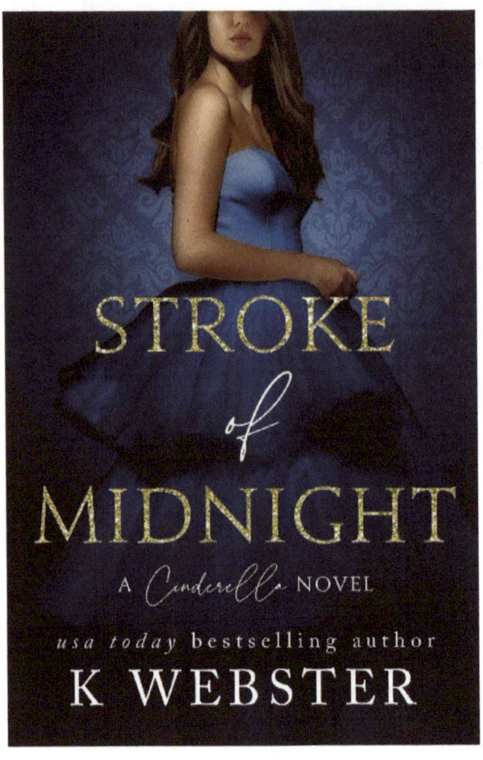

Excerpt from Stroke of Midnight by K. Webster

He reaches into his pocket to pull out his wallet. My eyes drift to the way it bulges with money. After he pulls the wad out, he sets it on the table.

"This belongs to you." He pushes the stack toward me. "For dinner."

I stare at the two thousand dollars we agreed upon. It doesn't feel real. Since meeting Winston, I've made over four thousand dollars, kicking me up to eleven grand in my college fund. It's annoying the relief I feel. It would have taken me months to make that much at FGM Services. I know Manda offered to pay, but I'd feel much better if I could somehow pay for it myself, even if it's just books and supplies. I hate having to be indebted to her.

I go to reach for the money, but his hand covers mine, stopping me. My heart does a nervous skip in my chest.

"Want to earn more?" His eyes flare with challenge.

I can do this.

I can endure his weird-ass fantasies because he pays well.

"Yes," I tell him with false bravado.

"Then wrap those lips around your breadstick. Lick it and suck it. Like you wish it were my dick." He nods at the bread on my plate. "Five hundred dollars."

God, he is so freaking bizarre.

I'm about to tell him where to shove his breadstick when I decide to negotiate for more. It's just a breadstick, not his dick. I can do this. Easily. I'm practically salivating for it anyway. The bread, not his dick.

"Eight," I counter.

"A grand if you moan my name while you do it and don't stop when Francis brings our food." He winks at me. "Easy money."

"Fifteen hundred and I'll gag on it."

He fists his hand, his jaw clenching, the first sign of a normal human reaction. Heat burns down my spine, pooling in my pelvis. I'm not turned on by him. Not a bit.

"You have yourself a deal."

WINSTON CONSTANTINE'S BREADSTICKS

FOR *STROKE OF MIDNIGHT* BY K. WEBSTER

Prep time: 10 min | Cooking time: 12 min | Total time: 22 min

Instructions

1. Preheat oven to 400 degrees Fahrenheit. Line a baking sheet with parchment paper. Set aside.
2. Unroll the puff pastry.
3. Add garlic powder, salt, and Mediterranean mix into the butter. Stir well and spread over the puff pastry.
4. Using a pizza wheel, cut into ½-inch strips. Separate and twist each piece. Place on the lined baking sheet.
5. Bake for 10-12 minutes or until golden. Allow to cool before removing from baking sheet.

Ingredients

1 sheet thawed puff pastry

1/4 cup butter, melted

1 teaspoon garlic powder

1/2 teaspoon salt

1 teaspoon Mediterranean mix (oregano, rosemary, salvia, thyme, basil, etc.)

From the author Corinne Michaels

Come Back for Me is not your normal second-chance romance…
    It comes with a twist!

TWICE-BAKED POTATOES WITH A TWIST

FOR *COME BACK FOR ME* BY CORINNE MICHAELS

This easy recipe puts a twist on the classic side
dish and will be sure to impress your guests!

🕐 **Prep Time: 10 min | Cook Time: 75 min | Yield: 4 servings**

Ingredients

- 4 large russet potatoes
- ¼ cup milk
- ¼ cup plain Greek yogurt
- ½ cup cotija cheese
- ½ cup feta cheese
- 1 teaspoon black pepper
- 1 teaspoon garlic powder
- ¾ teaspoon salt
- ¼ cup sliced green onions
- 2 tablespoons butter

Instructions

1. Preheat the oven to 400 degrees Fahrenheit and line a baking sheet with parchment paper.
2. Wash the potatoes, then pat dry with a paper towel.
3. Poke at least 8-10 holes in each potato using a fork or knife.
4. Place the potatoes on the prepared baking sheet and bake for 1 hour.
5. Allow the potatoes to cool for 10 minutes before cutting a thin layer off the top of each potato.
6. Use a spoon to carefully scoop out the inside of each potato, making sure not to break the potato skin.
7. Place the inside of the potatoes in a large bowl, then add the milk and plain Greek yogurt.
8. Use an electric mixer to thoroughly combine the ingredients until the potatoes are creamy and mashed.
9. Then, add the cotija cheese, feta cheese, pepper, garlic powder, and salt.
10. Beat again until smooth, then fill the potatoes with the mixture.
11. Bake again for 15 minutes, then cool for 10 minutes before garnishing with butter and green onions.

APPLE COLESLAW

FOR *THE BUTTERFLY EFFECT* BY KELLY ELLIOTT

Made with crunchy apples and carrots in a creamy mayonnaise dressing, this is one tasty recipe for a super easy salad. Just grate the apples and carrots, make the dressing, mix everything, and enjoy!

Ingredients

- 1 green apple
- 1 red apple
- 2 carrots
- 2 tablespoons mayonnaise
- 1 tablespoon apple cider vinegar
- salt and black pepper to taste
- 1 tablespoon chives, chopped

Instructions

1. In a large bowl, add mayonnaise, apple cider vinegar, black pepper and salt to taste. Stir well and set aside.
2. Grate the green apple, red apple, and carrots. Transfer into the bowl with the mayonnaise dressing. Stir well and chill for 30 minutes.
3. Sprinkle with chopped chives and serve!

From the author

Romance novels and good food have one thing in common that's undeniable: when they're good, they both leave me sated. I'm as obsessed with crime family novels as I am with Italian food and I can absolutely see my heroine making this dish to share with the family. Enjoy!

BRUSCHETTA

FOR *ALL HE'LL EVER BE* BY WILLOW WINTERS

Looking for an easy and delicious appetizer to
serve up on hot days? This bruschetta is the perfect
appetizer to munch on before the main course.

⏱ Prep Time: 10 min | Cook Time: 5 min | Inactive time: 30 min | Yield: 10 servings

Ingredients

For the tomato mixture

- 4 tablespoons extra virgin olive oil
- 3 cloves garlic, minced
- 4 large Roma tomatoes, diced
- 7-10 basil leaves, thinly sliced
- 1 tablespoon balsamic vinegar
- 1 teaspoon salt
- ¼ teaspoon crushed red pepper
- ¼ teaspoon pepper

For the bread

- 2 baguettes, sliced at a diagonal angle
- 2 tablespoons unsalted butter
- 2 cloves garlic, minced and crushed

Instructions

For the tomato mixture

1. Pour the olive oil into a pan and heat over medium-high heat.
2. Add the minced garlic and cook for 5 minutes until fragrant.
3. Remove from heat and allow to cool for at least 10 minutes.
4. While the garlic is cooling, add the diced tomatoes, basil leaves, balsamic vinegar, salt, red pepper, and pepper to a bowl.
5. Once the garlic has cooled, add the garlic and olive oil to the bowl.
6. Stir to combine, then marinate in the refrigerator for at least 30 minutes.

For the bread

1. Preheat the oven to 350 degrees Fahrenheit and line a baking sheet with parchment paper.
2. Place the slices of bread on the baking sheet.
3. Add the butter and garlic to a pan and cook for 5 minutes.
4. Brush the garlic butter over the bread, then cook for 10 minutes.
5. Allow the bread to cool for 5 minutes before placing the marinated bruschetta on top.
6. Garnish with more freshly sliced basil, then serve.

ANDIE'S CHEESE GRITS

FOR *MY CONE AND ONLY* BY SUSANNAH NIX

If you've never had cheese grits, prepare yourself…

⏱ **Prep Time: 10 min | Cook Time: 40 min | Yield: 6 servings**

Ingredients

3 cups whole milk

2 ½ cups lukewarm water

1 ½ cups corn grits

1 ½ teaspoons garlic powder

½ teaspoon smoked paprika

¼ teaspoon salt

¼ teaspoon cayenne pepper

½ cup unsalted butter

1 ½ cups sharp cheddar cheese, shredded

parsley for garnish

Instructions

1. Combine the milk and warm water in a pot, then bring to a boil.
2. Next, whisk in the corn grits until there are no lumps.
3. Stir in the garlic powder, smoked paprika, salt, and cayenne pepper.
4. Reduce the heat to low, cover with a lid, and simmer for 15 minutes.
5. Remove the lid, then whisk in the butter and cheese.
6. Turn off the heat, and serve the corn grits with fresh parsley.

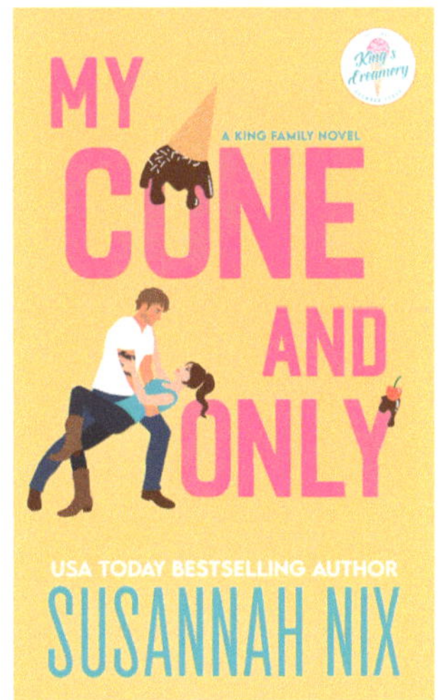

From the author Susannah Nix

These are the grits that inspired Wyatt to tell Andie he loved her in My Cone and Only, the first book in the King Family series. I'm not saying these cheesy grits are so good they'll make your brother's hot best friend fall at your feet and pledge his everlasting love to you— but they just might.

Excerpt from My Cone and Only

"With cheese?" Wyatt asked, his eyes lighting up. My mom's cheesy grits had been his favorite when we were kids. She'd taught me to make grits the old-fashioned way: low and slow with plenty of dairy fat. Good grits required patience and a cavalier attitude about your cholesterol levels.

PARMESAN BRUSSELS SPROUTS

FOR *DARK REIGN* BY AMELIA WILDE

Whoever declared war on Brussels sprouts clearly
hasn't tried these parmesan brussels!

Prep Time: 10 min | Cook Time: 15 min | Yield: 5 servings

Ingredients

- 2 pounds brussels sprouts
- 1 tablespoon olive oil
- 2 teaspoons balsamic vinegar
- 1 teaspoon thyme
- ½ teaspoon pepper
- ½ teaspoon salt
- 2 cups parmesan cheese

Instructions

1. Wash and cut the bottoms off of the brussels, then slice down the middle.
2. Add all of the halved brussels to a large bowl.
3. Season with olive oil, balsamic vinegar, thyme, pepper, and salt.
4. Toss with 1 ½ cups of parmesan cheese.
5. Then place the brussels in an air fryer for 15 minutes at 350 degrees Fahrenheit.
6. Toss the brussels halfway through 15 minutes to evenly cook them.
7. After 15 minutes, add the rest of the parmesan cheese and enjoy!

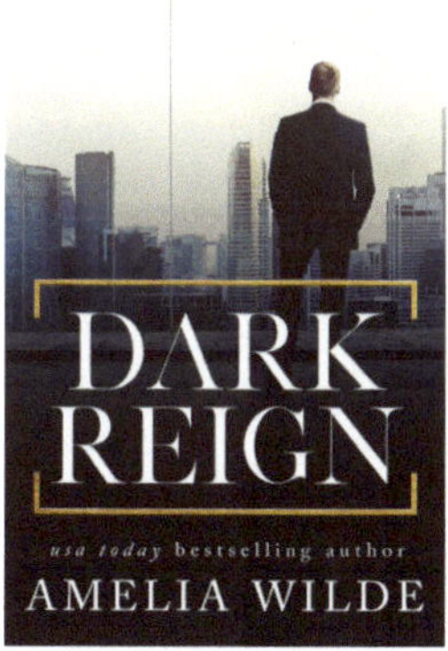

From the author

Daphne Morelli hates brussels sprouts until she meets her reclusive, rich hero, Emerson LeBlanc. He is the only person to both capture her heart and cook brussels sprouts in a way that tastes good to her.

SOUPS

From the author Amelia Wilde

Leo Morelli's favorite soup is butternut squash, which he prefers to eat in the wintertime. He loves it, but he loves Haley Constantine even more.

Excerpt from Secret Beast by Amelia Wilde

His spoon hovers over his bowl for a few moments. Then he lowers it again, brow furrowed.

"What hurts?"

Leo flicks his eyes up to mine. "Nothing."

"Liar. Tell me." The awkwardness cracks open and I take my first full breath of the evening.

He huffs out a sigh. "It's painful. To lift the spoon." I wait. "It feels different today."

The bullet wound. "I won't think less of you if you skip the soup."

His eyes flare and intensity floods back into the room, into my body. "I want the soup. It's my fucking favorite soup." Leo lets go of the spoon, his other hand coming up to rub his forehead, and there it is, at the surface—the toll of being shot. Of recovering. Of being in pain. "I can't do this."

I put my own spoon down, heart racing. "If you want to go back upstairs—"

"I can't let you think I take any pleasure in this."

"In dinner?"

"In keeping you captive."

LEO MORELLI'S BUTTERNUT SQUASH SOUP

FOR *SECRET BEAST* BY AMELIA WILDE

This easy recipe for butternut squash soup is healthy, creamy, full of flavor, and made with just a few simple ingredients. You will love the sweet, spiced flavor of this classic soup that's perfect for any time of the day.

Prep time: 15 min | Cooking time: 20 min | Total time: 35 min

Ingredients

1 tablespoon olive oil

1 onion, chopped

3 cloves garlic, minced

2 teaspoons grated fresh ginger

1 teaspoon sea salt, or to taste

1/4 teaspoon black pepper

1 teaspoon paprika powder

1 teaspoon fresh or dried thyme leaves, finely chopped

1 medium butternut squash, peeled and cut into 1-inch cubes

3 cups vegetable stock

1 1/2 cup coconut or soy milk

cream, chili flakes, and pine nuts for garnish

Instructions

1. Heat a large pot over medium heat. Add the olive oil.
2. Add the onion, garlic, ginger, salt, pepper, thyme, paprika, and squash. Sauté until the vegetables are soft. Stir frequently.
3. Add the vegetable stock and stir to combine. Add the lid to the pot and bring to a boil over medium-high heat.
4. Once the soup reaches a boil, turn the heat down to medium-low and simmer for about 5-10 minutes or until the butternut squash is very tender when you pierce it with a fork.
5. Remove the soup from the heat and add the milk.
6. Using an immersion blender, puree until smooth. Serve with cream, chili flakes, and pine nuts.

From the author Kennedy Ryan

From what I've ascertained (and I'm willing to be corrected!), the word gumbo finds its roots in Angola and/or Congo and translates from the word okra. Okra, one of the prominent ingredients in the soup, a staple of Cajun cuisine, first grew in Africa and was transported...transplanted to North America. Iris, the heroine of Long Shot, book 2 of my HOOPS series, hails from New Orleans, a city where so many influences, cultures, ethnicities, and backgrounds converge. Her family nicknames her Gumbo because her background, like the dish itself, is a blend of varied influences from all over the world. Like the plant, she has to be hardy, strong, and resilient no matter where she finds herself planted. Strength, dignity, and courage are the ingredients that make Iris the fighter, survivor, and woman she needs to be in every circumstance.

Excerpt from Long Shot by Kennedy Ryan

"There is a reservoir in my soul. A pool of strength, lying in wait. Like the Mississippi, it surges through my veins, cleansing me, renewing me, imbuing me with the power of a thousand priestesses. Lending me ancient courage born a thousand years before."

LONG SHOT GUMBO

FOR *LONG SHOT* BY KENNEDY RYAN

If you're looking for a hearty, southern-inspired meal, this gumbo is for you!

Prep Time: 20 min | Cook Time: 1 ½ hr | Yield: 6 servings

Ingredients

For the roux

1 cup all-purpose flour

2/3 cup canola oil

For the gumbo

1 tablespoon olive oil

12 ounces Andouille sausages, sliced

6 cups chicken stock

1 yellow onion, diced

2 cloves of garlic, minced

3 cups of celery, diced

1 green bell pepper, diced

¼ cup parsley, roughly chopped

2 tablespoons Cajun seasoning

1 tablespoon garlic powder

1 ½ teaspoons black pepper

¾ teaspoon salt

2 cups large deveined and deshelled shrimp, cooked

4 cups cooked chicken, shredded

3 cups white rice, cooked

¼ cup green onions

Instructions

For the roux

1. Combine the all-purpose flour and canola oil in a medium-size saucepan.
2. Cook on medium-low, stirring constantly for 45 minutes.
3. The result should be a caramel color, thick mixture.

For the gumbo

1. Add the olive oil to a large pot or Dutch oven and turn the heat to medium.
2. Then, add the sliced sausages and cook for 10-12 minutes.
3. Remove the sausages and set on a plate to the side.
4. Add ½ cup chicken stock and use a spatula to deglaze the pot.
5. Then, add the diced onion and sweat for five minutes until translucent.
6. Next, add the garlic, diced celery, green bell pepper, and roux to the pot.
7. Cook for five minutes, then add the rest of the chicken stock.
8. Add the parsley, then bring to a boil (skim off any foam on the top).
9. Reduce the heat to medium-low and add the Cajun seasoning, garlic powder, black pepper, and salt.
10. After 10 minutes, add the sausages, cooked shrimp, and shredded chicken.
11. Reduce the heat to low and stir in all the ingredients.
12. Then, cover and allow to sit for 15 minutes.
13. After 15 minutes, serve the gumbo over white rice and garnish with green onions.

From the author

Albóndigas is a comforting hearty Mexican soup that can be made on the stove, in a slow cooker, or in an Instant Pot. In Wicked Devil, the hero, Roman, makes it for our heroine and friends in an Instant Pot to help speed the process along, so you will find that recipe below, but if you'd prefer to make it on the stove, there will be alternative instructions for that method at the end.

ALBÓNDIGAS

FOR *WICKED DEVIL* BY DANIELA ROMERO

Ingredients

1 pound ground beef

½ cup uncooked white rice

1 white onion

1-2 celery stalks

1 can of corn

2 large carrots

3-5 russet potatoes

1 pound ground beef

1 can diced tomatoes

1 small serrano pepper

1 zucchini (optional)

salt and pepper to taste

flour tortillas

Instructions

1. In a separate bowl, combine your ground beef, rice, and 1 tablespoon of Caldo De Tomate.
2. Mix with hands until combined and set aside.
3. Peel potatoes and carrots and chop into bite-size pieces and place into a large Instant Pot cooking pot.
4. Dice celery, onion, and zucchini and add to your cooking pot.
5. Add in a can of corn (drained), and a can of diced tomatoes (undrained).
6. Slice and remove veins and seeds from the serrano pepper and then dice and add to your pot. For more heat, leave the seeds in.
7. Take your meat and rice mixture and form meatball-size rounds, using your hands to roll them into circular spheres and add to your Instant Pot.
8. Once all veggies and meat have been added, fill your pot with water, making sure not to pass the Instant Pot fill line while ensuring all of your vegetables are covered. Don't worry if the meatballs are not, they tend to float.
9. Stir in the remaining 4 tablespoons of Caldo De Tomate and then place your lid on, seal, and pressure cook on high for 14 minutes.
10. When the timer goes off, slow release and add salt and pepper to taste.
11. Warm your flour tortillas and eat along-side your albóndigas.

Alternative Stove-top Instructions

1. When cooking on a stove, the only change you will make is that you will sauté your serrano pepper, onion, carrots, and celery over medium heat in your soup pot until tender before adding your meatballs, potatoes, canned items, seasoning, and water.
2. Cook over medium heat or simmering, ensuring that your soup never comes to a full boil. It will take 35-45 minutes for the potatoes and meatballs to cook through, but if you allow it to simmer for an hour, your flavors will better develop.

3. Albóndigas is a soup that gets better with time when the flavors are allowed to rest and marry, so it will be ever more delicious the next day.
4. Notes and tips:
5. *If your broth feels bland depending on the amount of water added, stir in addition tablespoon of the Caldo De Tomate to deepen the flavor. Be sure to add 1 tablespoon at a time to ensure you don't oversalt the broth since the bouillon does contain a high salt content.

*Cilantro and fresh diced onion can be added as an optional garnish on top of your completed soup.

** 4-5 tablespoons Caldo De Tomate (Chicken and tomato bouillon found in the Hispanic aisle at your local grocer. If you can't find the chicken tomato bouillon, regular chicken bouillon will work fine as well.)

Excerpt from Escort by Skye Warren

"You can help me by chopping vegetables, if you'd like."

"Of course," she says, picking up an onion.

I take it away. "No need to make you cry so early in the evening. Start with the cauliflower."

That makes her laugh, and I feel myself relax. I have never cooked with a woman, certainly never a client, but we fall into a pattern of quiet preparation.

"Like this?" she asks, showing me the cherry tomatoes in quarters.

Her technique is clumsy, because this tiny kitchen leaves no room for cooking anything but the essentials. It reminds me of the way she kisses, all eagerness, no finesse. "Perfect," I say. "Keep going."

She flashes me a brief, nervous smile before turning back to work. My stomach feels lighter than it should, almost fluttery, and it takes me a moment to realize what this is: nerves. Dear God. She's turning me into a schoolboy.

It's perhaps with too much gusto that I break down the chicken, letting the slice of the knife break the strange tension in the air. The meat comes apart under my hands, tender and fragrant.

HARIRA SOUP

FOR *ESCORT* BY SKYE WARREN

Harira soup is a hearty tomato-based Moroccan soup made with legumes like lentils and chickpeas, fresh herbs, and warm spices including turmeric, cumin, ginger, and cinnamon. You will feel cozy while preparing and eating this fragrant soup, so gather all ingredients and get started!

Prep time: 10 min | Cook time: 50 min | Total time: 1 hr

Ingredients

2 tablespoons oil

1 onion, diced

3 stalks celery, diced

4 cloves garlic, minced

1 teaspoon ground cumin

1 teaspoon ground turmeric

1/2 teaspoon ground cinnamon

1/4 teaspoon ground ginger

1 can crushed tomatoes

1 tablespoon harissa, plus more for serving

8 cups vegetable stock or water

1 cup fresh cilantro or parsley, chopped, divided

1 cup lentils

1 can chickpeas, drained

salt to taste

Greek yogurt, lemon wedges, and toasted almonds to serve

Instructions

1. In a large heavy-bottomed soup pot or Dutch oven over medium-high heat, heat the oil and add the onion and celery. Cook, stirring occasionally, until the onion is translucent and softened, about 5 minutes.
2. Add the garlic, harissa, cumin, turmeric, cinnamon, and ginger. Continue to cook until fragrant and toasty, about 1 more minute.
3. Mix in the crushed tomatoes, harissa, stock, and half of the cilantro/parsley, and bring to a gentle boil. Reduce to a simmer and continue to cook, uncovered, for 15 minutes.
4. Add the lentils and chickpeas and season generously with salt. Cook for 30 more minutes, taste, and adjust harissa and seasonings as needed. Continue to cook until the lentils are soft. The soup should thicken, but if it gets too thick, add more stock or water as needed. Be sure to add extra salt along with the extra liquid.
5. Mix in and top with the remaining cilantro and serve warm with lemon wedges. Top with Greek yogurt and toasted almonds, if desired.

Ingredients

For the meatballs

½ pound lean ground beef

½ pound ground pork

½ cup breadcrumbs

¼ cup fresh parsley, chopped

½ cup crumbled feta cheese

1 room temperature egg

1 tablespoon olive oil

1 teaspoon black pepper

1 teaspoon oregano

¾ teaspoon salt

For the soup

1 tablespoon olive oil

1 white onion, diced

3 cloves garlic, minced

1 cup carrots, roughly chopped

1 cup celery, chopped

2 teaspoons fresh parsley, chopped

1 teaspoon oregano

½ teaspoon pepper

½ teaspoon salt

4 cups vegetable broth

1 ½ cups orzo pasta

4 cups fresh spinach

feta cheese for garnish

fresh parsley for garnish

WEDDING SOUP

FOR *CAPTIVE BRIDE* BY ALTA HENSLEY

This might just be the BEST wedding soup out there! Full of rich flavor, this soup is the perfect comfort food.

⏱ **Prep Time: 25 min | Cook Time: 60 min | Yield: 6 servings**

Instructions

For the meatballs

1. Preheat oven to 350 degrees Fahrenheit and line a baking sheet with parchment paper.
2. Add the beef, pork, breadcrumbs, parsley, feta cheese, egg, olive oil, black pepper, oregano, and salt to a large mixing bowl.
3. Use your hands to combine the ingredients, then shape into 1 ½-inch meatballs.
4. Place the meatballs on the prepared baking sheet, and bake for 25-30 minutes, rotating halfway.
5. After the meatballs have browned, remove them from the oven and allow them to cool.

For the soup

1. Add the tablespoon of olive oil and diced onion to a Dutch oven or large pot.
2. Cook the onion over medium-high heat, stirring occasionally, for five minutes until translucent.
3. Then, add the minced garlic and cook for two minutes, or until aromatic.
4. Next, add the carrots, celery, parsley, oregano, pepper, and salt.
5. Allow the vegetables to cook for 10 minutes before adding the vegetable broth.
6. Bring the mixture to a boil, then add the orzo pasta.
7. Reduce the heat to medium, cover, and cook for 8-10 minutes until the pasta is done.
8. Finally, reduce the heat to low and add in the spinach and meatballs.
9. Allow the soup to simmer on low for 10 minutes before serving
10. Finally, garnish with crumbled feta cheese and fresh parsley.

MAIN DISHES

From the author

I grew up hearing stories about my mother and grandparents in Indonesia, but I never found an Indonesian-American heroine in a romance. Then I realized that I had the power to change that. So I wrote Overture, a taboo romance featuring a violin prodigy and the man who protects her.

FRIED TOFU WITH INDONESIAN PEANUT SAUCE

FOR *OVERTURE* BY SKYE WARREN

This air-fried tofu with Indonesian peanut sauce is the perfect meal to enjoy when you're looking for something unique, delicious, and easy to make!

Prep Time: 20 min | Cook Time: 40 min | Yield: 4 servings

Ingredients

1 cup jasmine rice

1 can coconut milk

1 block extra firm tofu

½ cup rice flour

1 teaspoon turmeric

½ teaspoon ground ginger

½ cup water

1/3 cup crunchy peanut butter

1 ½ tablespoons soy sauce

1 tablespoon chili garlic paste

1 tablespoon grated ginger

3 teaspoons lime juice

2 teaspoons tamarind, pureed

1 teaspoon sambal oelek

1 teaspoon palm sugar

1 large carrot, sliced thinly

½ Lebanese cucumber, sliced

1 cup bean sprouts, trimmed and washed

¼ cup green onions, diced

2 tablespoons peanuts, finely chopped

2 tablespoons fresh cilantro, roughly chopped

1 tablespoon sesame seeds

Instructions

1. Add the rice and coconut milk to a small saucepan, then bring to a boil.
2. Reduce the heat to medium-low, cover, and allow to cook for 15 minutes.
3. After 15 minutes, remove the lid and fluff with a fork, then set to the side.
4. To remove any excess water from the tofu, wrap with 5 paper towels, then place on a cutting board with a heavy object on top of the tofu for 10 minutes.
5. After, use a knife to cut into bite-size pieces.
6. In a small bowl, combine the flour, turmeric, and ground ginger.
7. Toss the tofu pieces in the flour mixture, then place in the air fryer at 350 degrees Fahrenheit for 15 minutes.
8. While the tofu is cooking, start on the peanut sauce by adding the water, crunchy peanut butter, soy sauce, and chili garlic paste to a saucepan.
9. Whisk to combine the ingredients, then heat over medium heat.
10. Next, add the grated ginger, lime juice, tamarind, sambal oelek, and palm sugar.

TEXAS BBQ TACOS

FOR *THE WRIGHT BROTHER* BY K.A. LINDE

You NEED these pulled chicken tacos with
homemade Texas BBQ sauce in your life!

Prep Time: 30 min | Cook Time: 45 min | Inactive Time: 120 min | Yield: 8 servings

Ingredients

For the BBQ sauce

1 tablespoon olive oil

2 tablespoons unsalted butter

½ red onion, diced

3 garlic cloves, minced

1 can tomato paste

1 ½ cups water

½ cup brown sugar

¼ cup molasses

¼ cup applesauce

¼ cup honey

¼ cup apple cider vinegar

3 tablespoons cornstarch

2 tablespoons lemon juice

2 tablespoons Worcestershire sauce

2 tablespoons Dijon mustard

2 tablespoons chili powder

1 tablespoon paprika

2 teaspoons black pepper

1 teaspoon smoked cherry salt

1 teaspoon garlic powder

1 teaspoon cumin

For the chicken tacos

3 chicken breasts

1 tablespoon olive oil

1 tablespoon lime juice

2 teaspoons pepper

1 teaspoon salt

8-12 corn tortillas

For the coleslaw

½ cup green cabbage, shredded

½ cup purple cabbage, shredded

½ cup carrots, peeled and shredded

¼ cup jalapenos, diced

¼ cup fresh cilantro, diced

¼ cup mayonnaise

1 tablespoon cane sugar

1 tablespoon lemon juice

1 tablespoon rice wine vinegar

¼ teaspoon salt

Instructions

For the BBQ sauce

1. Add the olive oil and butter to a large pot or Dutch oven.
2. Heat over medium heat until melted, then add the diced red onion.
3. Sweat for 5 minutes until translucent, then add the minced garlic and cook for 2-3 minutes.
4. Next, add the tomato paste and stir to coat the onion and garlic.
5. Then, add the water, brown sugar, molasses, honey, applesauce, and apple cider vinegar.
6. Stir to combine, and increase the heat to medium-high.
7. After, add the cornstarch to thicken the BBQ sauce.
8. Stir until the BBQ sauce has thickened up, about 5-7 minutes.
9. Add the lemon juice, Worcestershire sauce, Dijon mustard, chili powder, paprika, black pepper, cherry salt, garlic powder, and cumin.
10. Stir in the ingredients, then reduce the heat to low and cover.
11. Allow the BBQ sauce to simmer for two hours, stirring every 20-30 minutes.
12. After two hours, remove the sauce from the heat and allow to cool before adding 1 cup to the pulled chicken breasts.

For the chicken tacos

1. Preheat the oven to 400 degrees Fahrenheit and line a large baking sheet with parchment paper.
2. Pat the chicken breasts dry with a paper towel, then season with the olive oil, lime juice, pepper, and salt.
3. Place the chicken on the prepared baking sheet and bake for 30 minutes.
4. After 30 minutes, allow to cool for 10 minutes.
5. Then, place the chicken breasts in a large bowl and use two forks to pull the chicken breasts until the meat has reached your desired consistency.
6. Add one cup of the Texas BBQ sauce to the chicken and use tongs to evenly coat.
7. Toast the corn tortillas, then add the BBQ pulled chicken.

For the coleslaw

1. Add your shredded green and purple cabbage, carrots, diced jalapenos, and cilantro to a medium-size bowl.
2. In another bowl, combine the mayonnaise, sugar, lemon juice, rice wine vinegar, and salt.
3. Stir until smooth, then pour the dressing over the coleslaw.
4. Use tongs or a fork to evenly distribute the dressing.
5. Then, add the coleslaw to the top of the pulled chicken tacos and enjoy!

The
WRIGHT
BROTHER
What's Wright is Right.
USA Today bestselling author
K.A. LINDE

ONE-POT LASAGNA

FOR *FAKE* BY KYLIE SCOTT

Do you know what's better than a hearty and delicious lasagna? A one-pot lasagna that makes cleanup a breeze!

🕐 **Prep Time: 30 min | Cook Time: 60 min | Yield: 10 servings**

Ingredients

For the lasagna

2 tablespoons olive oil

1 white onion, diced

3 cloves garlic, minced

1 can tomato paste

1 cup plum tomatoes, roughly chopped

¼ cup vegetable broth

1 pound ground beef

¼ cup dry red wine, like Merlot

2 tablespoons oregano

1 tablespoon dried basil

3 teaspoons black pepper

2 teaspoons salt

1 box lasagna sheets

1 cup mozzarella cheese

fresh basil for garnish

grated parmesan for garnish

For the cheese mixture

2 cups ricotta cheese

1 cup parmesan cheese

1 tablespoon dried rosemary

1 tablespoon olive oil

Instructions

1. Preheat the oven to 425 degrees Fahrenheit, then add the olive oil to a large cast iron skillet.
2. Turn the heat to medium-high and allow the skillet to heat up for roughly 5 minutes.
3. Once the skillet is warm, add the diced onion and cook for 5 minutes until translucent.
4. Next, add the minced garlic and tomato paste, stirring to coat.
5. Sauté for three minutes until aromatic, then add the plum tomatoes and vegetable broth.
6. After cooking for five minutes, add the ground beef, red wine, oregano, dried basil, pepper, and salt.
7. Cook until the meat is lightly browned, about 7 minutes.
8. Then, move the meat mixture to one side and add two sheets of lasagna to the bottom of the cast iron skillet.
9. Next, spread a hearty helping of the cheese mixture over the lasagna sheets.
10. Then, cover that with the meat and repeat on the other side of the pot.
11. Continue steps 8–9 as you make your way to the top of the pot.

NOTE: Not all of the lasagna sheets need to be used, just distribute evenly.

12. Once the final layer has been added, spread the mozzarella cheese evenly over the top and then cover with aluminum foil.
13. Bake for 40 minutes covered, 10 minutes uncovered, and finally broil for 3-4 minutes.
14. Allow to cool for at least 10 minutes.
15. Top with fresh basil and grated parmesan cheese, then serve up!

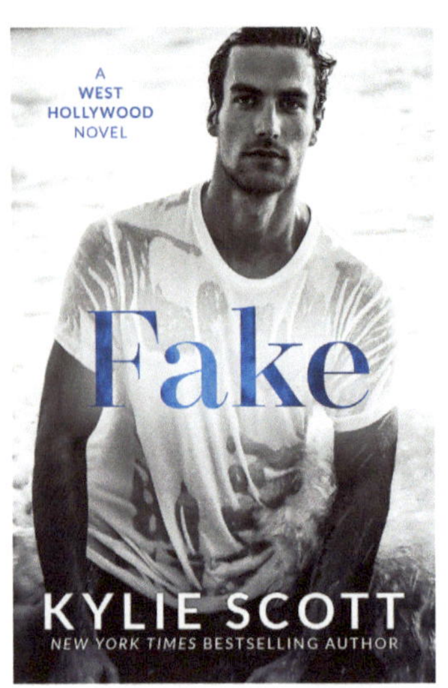

From the author Kylie Scott

One of the great loves of my life will always be carbohydrates. And what better way to indulge than with pasta! Combine this with my innate laziness as we minimize on the cleanup by only using one dish and you have a recipe for a perfect Happy Ever After. Best enjoyed with a great beer or a bottle of red.

Excerpt from Unconditional by QB Tyler

"Shit," I hear from the kitchen followed by the slam of a microwave. I'd whipped up some stir-fry while he was gone, knowing he'd be hungry when he got back, and I assume that's what he's trying to do. I sit up, throwing the blanket off of me and pad into the kitchen where I see him sitting at the table with his head in his hands and a tumbler of a brown liquid—probably whiskey—in front of him.

"Rough night?" I ask. His head snaps up and you'd think I was naked by the way he looks over my body. I'm wearing a sweatshirt and leggings, so it's not like he has flesh to feast his eyes upon. I look down to see, feeling slightly subconscious, but when I meet his eyes, they're filled with something I don't recognize.

Want maybe?

"Not as rough as this afternoon," he grumbles.

"I'm so sorry that it was so hard for you. I won't give you the arduous task of having to kiss me again, swear." I was tired of his moody teenage-girl attitude.

That's my role.

Instead, I'm handling this with way more maturity, making me wonder who exactly the adult is here. I move towards the microwave and open the door, knowing that he always leaves it in there too long and sure enough his food is practically steaming.

The plate is hot and I snatch my hand back from it, the heat searing into my skin and shooting up my arm. "Fuck," I groan as I wave my hand to try and cool my fingers. He's by my side instantly, pulling my hand to the sink and letting it run under the cool water which does nothing for my heated skin that's responding to his touch. "You always leave it in there too long."

"Sorry." He pulls my fingers out from under the water and holds them in his hand before pulling the wet hand to his lips, sucking the excess water from my skin. He presses kisses to each of my burnt fingertips before letting it gently fall. "Better?"

From the author

Stir-fry pairs well with whiskey and bad decisions. Add the *spice* as you see fit!

VEGETABLE STIR-FRY

FOR *UNCONDITIONAL* BY QB TYLER

This vegetable stir-fry is a great mixture of colorful vegetables, sautéed in a sweet and savory sauce that makes for a simple weeknight meal! It takes just 15 minutes to make from start to finish! You will definitely be in love with this dish!

Prep time: 10 min | Cook time: 5 min | Total time: 15 min

Ingredients

1 tablespoon olive oil

1 red bell pepper, sliced

1 green bell pepper, sliced

1 cup carrots, sliced

1 cup mushrooms, sliced

2 cups broccoli florets

1 cup baby corn

¼ cup soy sauce

3 cloves garlic, minced

1 tablespoon coconut sugar

1 teaspoon sesame oil

1/2 cup vegetable stock

1 tablespoon cornstarch

chopped green onions for garnish

sesame seeds for garnish

Instructions

1. In a wok or large skillet over medium-high heat, add olive oil. Add bell peppers, carrots, mushrooms, broccoli, and baby corn. Sauté 2-3 minutes until veggies are almost tender.
2. In a small bowl, whisk together soy sauce, garlic, coconut sugar, sesame oil, vegetable stock, and cornstarch.
3. Pour over veggies and cook until the sauce has thickened.
4. Garnish with chopped green onions and sesame seeds if desired. Enjoy!

MICI

FOR *BIG BAD WOLF* BY JENIKA SNOW

Mici are the delicious, beer-soaked sausages that you never knew you needed!

Prep Time: 20 min | Cook Time: 45 min | Inactive Time: 2-4 hr | Yield: 8 servings

Ingredients

1 pound ground beef

1 pound ground pork

1 tablespoon garlic powder

2 teaspoons thyme

1 teaspoon salt

1 teaspoon cumin

½ teaspoon black pepper

¼ teaspoon cayenne pepper

a pinch of cinnamon

½ cup beef stock

¼ cup beer

1 teaspoon baking soda

fresh parsley for garnish

Instructions

1. Place the ground beef and pork in a large mixing bowl.
2. Then, season with garlic powder, thyme, salt, cumin, black pepper, cayenne pepper, and cinnamon.
3. Use your hands or a wooden spoon to combine until thoroughly mixed.
4. Next, add the beef stock, beer, and baking soda.
5. Mix into the meat mixture with a spoon, then refrigerate for one hour.
6. After one hour, drain any liquid, wet your hands, and form the meat into thin sausages.
7. Place the sausages on a prepared baking tray, then refrigerate for at least one hour.
8. Preheat the oven to 375 degrees Fahrenheit.
9. Place the baking sheet with the sausages in the oven for 45 minutes, rotating the sausages halfway.
10. Allow them to cool, then garnish with fresh parsley.
11. Serve with yellow mustard, ketchup, and a nice beer!

From the author

At times called the "national dish of Romania," mici is a staple picnic and BBQ item, and in recent times, has been strongly associated with the national holiday, *International Worker's Day*.

"As long as you have the love of food to share, anyone and everyone can come together as a unit over cooking and eating."

Ingredients

For the burgers

- 1 pound lean ground beef
- ¾ teaspoon black pepper
- ½ teaspoon garlic powder
- ¼ teaspoon salt
- ½ cup crumbled blue cheese
- 2 tablespoons olive oil

For the toppings

- 3 tablespoons butter
- 3 cloves garlic, minced
- 8 slider brioche buns
- 2 Roma tomatoes, sliced
- ½ cup crumbled blue cheese
- ½ cup pickles
- lettuce, optional
- ketchup, optional

BLUE CHEESE BURGER SLIDERS

FOR *THE PERFECT FIRST* BY MAYA HUGHES

Sliders: the cute mini hamburgers that you can eat four of without feeling guilty. These blue cheese burger sliders are the perfect appetizer to serve up!

Prep Time: 30 min | Cook Time: 20 min | Yield: 8 servings

Instructions

For the burgers

1. In a medium-size bowl, combine the lean ground beef, pepper, garlic powder, and salt.
2. Roll into 8 balls.
3. Then poke a hole in the burger meat and place blue cheese in the middle.
4. Cover the hole, then flatten into a patty-shape.
5. Add the olive oil to a cast iron skillet and turn the heat to medium.
6. Once the skillet is hot, add the patty and cook for 2-3 minutes on each side.
7. Repeat with all the patties, then set to the side.

For the toppings

1. Preheat the oven to 350 degrees Fahrenheit and line a baking sheet with parchment paper.
2. Add the butter and minced garlic to a small pan.
3. Cook over medium heat for 2-3 minutes until the garlic is golden.
4. Slice the buns in half, then brush the garlic butter over the inside of the buns.
5. Place the buns on the baking sheet and bake for 7 minutes until golden and crunchy.
6. Then, layer the tomato on the buns before topping with the patties, blue cheese, and pickles.
7. Add lettuce or ketchup (if you want), then serve and enjoy.

WHISKEY-BASED BBQ SAUCE WITH RIBS

FOR *ON THE ROCKS* BY KANDI STEINER

There are few things better than ribs that fall right off the bone. These ribs with a whiskey-based BBQ sauce are totally drool-worthy.

Prep Time: 30 min | Cook Time: 3 hr | Inactive Time: 2 hr | Yield: 10 servings

Ingredients

For the BBQ sauce

1 tablespoon olive oil

½ white onion, diced

4 garlic cloves, minced

½ can tomato paste

1 cup bourbon whiskey

½ cup ketchup

¼ cup brown sugar

¼ cup molasses

¼ cup red wine vinegar

3 tablespoons cornstarch

2 tablespoons Worcestershire sauce

2 tablespoons cumin

2 tablespoons smoked paprika

1 teaspoon cayenne pepper

1 teaspoon salt

2 teaspoons garlic powder

For the ribs

¼ cup brown sugar

2 tablespoons black pepper

1 tablespoon cumin

1 tablespoon smoked paprika

1 teaspoon cayenne pepper

1 teaspoon salt

1 teaspoon garlic powder

1 teaspoon dry mustard

1 rack of ribs, 12 ribs

green onions for garnish

coleslaw for a side dish, optional

Instructions

For the BBQ sauce

1. In a large pot, add the olive oil and heat for 2 minutes until the pot is warm.
2. Next, add the diced onion and sweat for 5 minutes.
3. Then, add the minced garlic and tomato paste, stirring to coat.
4. After 2-3 minutes, pour in the whiskey, ketchup, brown sugar, molasses, and red wine vinegar.
5. Stir the mixture, then pour in the cornstarch and stir for 5 minutes.
6. Add the Worcestershire sauce, cumin, paprika, pepper, salt, and garlic powder.
7. Stir, then reduce the heat to low and allow to simmer for 30 minutes.
8. After 30 minutes, remove the pot from heat.
9. Then, use an immersion blender or pour the sauce into a blender to puree.
10. Puree until smooth, then add back to the pot and set to the side.

For the ribs

1. Preheat the oven to 250 degrees Fahrenheit and place aluminum foil in a 9-by-13 baking dish.
2. In a small bowl, mix the brown sugar, pepper, cumin, smoked paprika, cayenne pepper, salt, garlic powder, and dry mustard.
3. Then pour the dry rub over the ribs, making sure to coat both sides evenly.
4. Place the ribs, meat side down, on the foil-lined baking dish and prick 5-8 holes in the back of ribs.
5. Fold the foil over the ribs and cook for two hours.
6. After two hours, pull the ribs out to cool for 15 minutes and increase the oven temperature to 350 degrees Fahrenheit.
7. After the ribs have cooled, open the foil, and drain the fat, then pour 1 cup of the BBQ sauce over the ribs.
8. Place the ribs meat side up with the foil open and bake for 15 minutes.
9. Then, brush another layer of BBQ sauce over the top and bake for another 15 minutes.
10. Repeat steps 8-9 two more times, then turn off the oven and allow the ribs to cool outside the foil for 20 minutes before serving.

From the character Noah Becker

"Dad was known around the distillery and the whole town for his famous bourbon barbecue sauce. Mom might kill me if she finds out I'm sharing it, but after making these ribs for Ruby Grace one warm summer evening, she said it'd be a crime to keep the recipe all to myself. I think it'd make Dad proud, too—knowing his special sauce lives on in his absence. For an added delight, pair these ribs with some sweet coleslaw—Mama's favorite."

From the author Kandi Steiner

Nothing says Becker Brothers like bourbon and barbecue. Enjoy this delicious sauce while you fall in love with Noah, Logan, Mikey, and Jordan—and help them solve the mystery of their father's death along the way.

HAWAIIAN KALUA PORK

FOR *FINDING ELODIE* BY SUSAN STOKER

Kalua pork has never been so easy to make!

🕐 **Prep Time: 20 min | Cook Time: 10 hr | | Yield: 12 servings**

Ingredients

- 1 4-pound pork shoulder
- 1 tablespoon Hickory liquid smoke
- 1 tablespoon smoked cherry salt
- 2 teaspoons salt
- 1 teaspoon black pepper
- ½ cup beef stock, if needed

Instructions

1. Pat the pork shoulder dry with paper towels, then place in a slow cooker.
2. Season with the liquid smoke, smoked cherry salt, salt, and black pepper.
3. Place the lid on top of the slow cooker, and cook on low for 10 hours.
4. After 10 hours, remove the pork from the slow cooker and place in a large bowl.
5. Use a fork to remove any fatty pieces.
6. Then, shred with a fork and return to the pot once the whole shoulder is shredded.
7. If there isn't any liquid left in the slow cooker, add ½ cup of beef stock.
8. Keep warm until ready to serve, then enjoy!

From the author

In my SEAL Team Hawaii series, I spend a lot of time talking about the amazing Hawaiian food. My couples all take great pleasure in eating Hawaiian meals together. In Finding Elodie, my main characters bond over kalua pig, short ribs, and of course malasadas! Enjoy!

PUB BURGER

FOR *SILVER BREWER* BY L.B. DUNBAR

Who's ready for a burger? This pub burger with
caramelized onions, smoked aged cheddar cheese,
and a garlic rosemary aioli is calling your name.

🕐 **Prep Time: 10 min | Cook Time: 45 min | Yield: 4 servings**

Ingredients

For the onions

1 white onion, sliced

½ cup unsalted butter

1 tablespoon Worcestershire sauce

1 teaspoon black pepper

¼ teaspoon salt

For the burger

1 pound ground beef

1 teaspoon black pepper

1 teaspoon salt

1 tablespoon olive oil

4 slices smoked aged cheddar cheese

4 brioche or potato buns

2 Roma tomatoes, sliced

1 head of escarole lettuce, chopped

¼ cup of pickles

For the garlic rosemary aioli

½ cup mayonnaise

6 cloves garlic, diced

2 tablespoons dried rosemary

2 tablespoons lemon juice

1 teaspoon black pepper

¼ teaspoon salt

Instructions

For the onions

1. Add the butter to a large pan and heat over medium heat.
2. Once the butter has almost completely melted, reduce the heat to medium-low and add the sliced onion.
3. Use a spatula to continuously move the onions around to prevent burning.
4. After 10 minutes, add the Worcestershire sauce, pepper, and salt.
5. Continue cooking until the onions are golden and soft.
6. Set the onions to the side.

For the burger

1. In a medium bowl, combine the ground beef, pepper, and salt.
2. Form into four equal-size patties.
3. Pour the olive oil on a cast iron skillet or pan, then allow to heat for 3 minutes until hot.
4. Place the patties on the cast iron skillet, cooking for 4 minutes over medium-high heat on one side.
5. Flip the patties and add one slice of the cheese to the top of each patty.
6. After 3-4 minutes, remove the patties from the heat and set them to the side.
7. Next, slice the buns in half and toast them in an air fryer or toaster until golden.
8. To assemble your burger, add 2-3 pieces of the escarole lettuce to the bottom of the bun, then add the caramelized onion slices.
9. Next, top with the burger and melted cheese.
10. Finally, add the tomato and pickles.
11. Before putting the top of the bun on the burger, remember to add the rosemary aioli.

For the aioli

1. Add the mayonnaise, minced garlic, dried rosemary, lemon juice, pepper, and salt to a blender.
2. Blend until smooth, about two minutes.
3. Add a spoonful to the burger, then place the bun on top and enjoy.

Excerpt from Silver Brewer, from the point of view of Giant

"Ax throwing, laughing, even a foiled attempt at flipping a burger over an open flame. Letty is a metaphor for life, and I want to live her."

EASY GRILL STEAK NIGHT

Ingredients

4 New York strip steaks approximately 8 ounces each

1/2 tablespoon red pepper

1/2 tablespoon garlic powder

1/2 tablespoon onion powder

1/4 teaspoon paprika

½ tablespoon canola or vegetable oil

salt and pepper to taste

Instructions

1. Mix black pepper, coarse salt, red pepper, garlic powder, onion powder, paprika, and vegetable or canola oil together.
2. Liberally season steaks with mixture.
3. Let the steaks sit at room temperature for 1 hour.
4. Preheat indoor or outdoor grill.
5. Cook for 3-4 minutes per side until golden brown or until the thermometer registers 145 degrees Fahrenheit for a medium steak (warm pink center), 150 degrees Fahrenheit for a medium-well steak (slightly pink center), or 160 degrees Fahrenheit for a well-done steak (little or no pink).
6. Remove from the grill once desired temperature is achieved. Let the steak rest for 5 minutes and then serve immediately.
7. To check the temperature, remove the steak from the grill. Insert thermometer through the side of steak, tip in the center, not touching bone or fat.

FOREVER TUNA CASSEROLE

FOR *FOREVER RIGHT NOW* BY EMMA SCOTT

This ultimate comfort food dish is just what you need!

Prep Time: 15 min | Cook Time: 30 min | Yield: 12 servings

Ingredients

24 ounces wide egg noodles, cooked

18 ounces canned tuna, drained

2 cans condensed cream of mushroom soup

2 cups frozen peas

2 cups parmesan cheese

½ cup milk

½ cup breadcrumbs

½ cup butter, melted

1 teaspoon garlic powder

1 teaspoon black pepper

½ teaspoon salt

fresh parsley for garnish

Instructions

1. Preheat oven to 375 degrees Fahrenheit and grease a 9-by-13 casserole dish.
2. Add the cooked egg noodles to the casserole dish.
3. In a large bowl, combine the canned tuna, condensed cream of mushroom soup, frozen peas, 1 cup of parmesan cheese, and milk.
4. Mix together, then pour over the egg noodles, and use a spoon to evenly distribute and coat the egg noodles.
5. In a small bowl, combine the rest of the parmesan cheese, the breadcrumbs, melted butter, garlic powder, black pepper, and salt.
6. Sprinkle over the tuna casserole, then bake for 20 minutes.
7. Broil on low for 30 minutes until the top is slightly crispy and golden.
8. Finally, garnish with fresh parsley and enjoy!

Forever Right Now
a novel
Emma Scott
Author of The Full Tilt Duet
and The Butterfly Project

From the author

In *Forever Right Now,* recovering addict Darlene moves into a San Francisco Victorian where Sawyer, a single dad, is struggling to finish law school and retain custody of his baby daughter, Olivia. The tuna casserole, a dish that Darlene makes, is a symbol of comfort, and brings people together—first her and Sawyer when she makes it for him (because he's too overworked and tired to cook for himself), and later, when the parents of Olivia's mom come to fight for custody. The dish seems simple and plain, but there's a lot of love and warmth in it, and brings out the love and warmth in the characters too.

Excerpt from Forever Right Now by Emma Scott

I started to pack up my materials into my briefcase. A soft knock came at the door.

I opened it to Darlene.

She wasn't wearing that dance top but a peach-colored sundress, no shoes. The dress skimmed her breasts and flared out at her narrow waist. Her hair fell over her shoulders, dark with dampness from a recent shower. Oven mitts covered her hands to protect them from the glass pan she held. The delicious scent of tuna casserole wafted up from underneath the tinfoil. It smelled warm and good in a way my TV dinners never did.

"I know it's late, but I took a chance that you were up," she said. "I made another casserole. Mostly because it's the only thing I know how to make. And to keep myself out of trouble."

She seemed on the verge of tears for a second, but blinked them away to smile brightly. "Anyway, this is for you. Can I just drop it off? Then I'll go."

"Uh, sure," I said, opening the door for her. "Thanks."

"I don't want it to go to waste." She breezed past me and set it on the kitchen counter. "You can return the pan whenever."

"Are you okay?" I asked.

"Sure. Great. I don't want to bother you. I should go back…" She headed for the door, head down and her voice thick. "Livvie's asleep? Of course, it's late…"

"Darlene, what's wrong?"

"It's nothing. Stupid, really." At my door, she took off the oven mitts and tucked them under her arm. "I just had some kind of good news today and I wanted to tell somebody. At eleven thirty at night," she said with a small laugh. "Sorry, never mind. I don't want to bother you."

She turned to leave and I knew I'd never sleep that night if I let her.

Excerpt from Let's Get Textual by Teagan Hunter

"I bought you dinner, Delia. We're past the nerves stage. We're two friends enjoying a show together, eating hot wings—or in your case, wimpy wings."

"Did you just mock my taste in wings?"

"Am I wrong?" he questions.

"I…YES! Those things are spicy!"

"To who? A toddler?"

"You're mean, Zach."

"And you enjoy it, Delia."

SPICY BONELESS WINGS

FOR *LET'S GET TEXTUAL* BY TEAGAN HUNTER

Are you ready for these air-fried sweet and
spicy boneless chicken wings?

Prep Time: 15 min | Cook Time: 30 min | Inactive Time: 1 hr | Yield: 4 servings

Ingredients

For the wings

2 large boneless, skinless chicken
breasts

1 ½ cups all-purpose flour

1 teaspoon smoked cherry salt

1 teaspoon garlic powder

¾ teaspoon ground black pepper

½ teaspoon smoked paprika

¼ teaspoon cayenne pepper

1 cup milk

1 tablespoon lemon juice

1 egg, room temperature

For the sauce

1 cup brown sugar

¼ cup hot sauce

2 tablespoons honey

2 tablespoons water

1 tablespoon Worcestershire sauce

Instructions

For the wings

1. Pat the chicken breasts dry, then cut into large pieces.
2. In one bowl, combine the flour, cherry salt, garlic powder, pepper, paprika, and cayenne pepper.
3. In another bowl, combine the milk and lemon juice.
4. Allow the milk mixture to sit for 5 minutes, then whisk in one egg.
5. Double-coat the chicken pieces by dipping them in the milk, then the flour, back into the milk mixture, and finish with the flour.
6. Repeat with all the chicken pieces, then place in the refrigerator for one hour.
7. After an hour, cook the chicken in an air fryer at 380 degrees Fahrenheit for 25 minutes, tossing halfway.
8. Once cooked, place in a bowl and set to the side.

For the sauce

1. In a saucepan, combine all of the ingredients and bring to a simmer.
2. Once combined, remove from heat and allow to cool for 5 minutes.
3. Pour the mixture over the wings and use metal tongs to evenly coat the chicken in the sauce.

Ingredients

1. 2 tablespoons olive oil
2. 4 bacon strips, cut
3. 4 chicken thighs
4. 4 chicken drumsticks
5. 3 teaspoons salt
6. 3 teaspoons black pepper
7. 1 ½ cups red wine
8. 1 white onion, diced
9. 4 cloves garlic, minced
10. 2 cups carrots, peeled and chopped
11. 1 ¼ cups chicken broth
12. 10 sprigs fresh thyme
13. 4 tablespoons butter, sliced
14. 1 ½ cups cherry tomatoes
15. 1 ½ cups cremini mushrooms, sliced
16. 2 tablespoons parsley, for garnish

COQ AU VIN

FOR *TEARS OF TESS* BY PEPPER WINTERS

Say hello to this French classic! This easy recipe
cooks chicken thighs and drumsticks in wine and
yields tender meat that falls off the bone!

Prep Time: 30 min | Cook Time: 60 min | Yield: 8 servings

Instructions

1. Preheat the oven to 350 degrees Fahrenheit.
2. In a large Dutch oven, add the olive oil and sliced bacon.
3. Cook the bacon over medium heat for 8 minutes, then remove from the pot and place on a plate to the side.
4. Pat the chicken thighs and drumsticks dry, then season with 1 teaspoon of salt and pepper.
5. Add a splash of the red wine to deglaze the pot, then add the seasoned chicken thighs and drumsticks.
6. Cook the chicken for about 10 minutes, or until lightly golden and no longer pink.
7. Remove the chicken from the pot, and add another splash of red wine to deglaze again.
8. Next, add the diced onion and sweat for 5 minutes on medium heat until translucent before adding the minced garlic and carrots.
9. Add the rest of the salt and pepper to the vegetables, and cook for 10 minutes until the carrots are tender.
10. Pour in the rest of the wine, then add the chicken broth and fresh thyme.
11. Place the bacon and chicken back in the pot and allow to simmer for 10 minutes.
12. Then, add the sliced butter, cherry tomatoes, and mushrooms to the pot.
13. Cover with the lid and cook in the oven for 30 minutes.
14. Garnish with fresh parley, serve over mashed potatoes or polenta, and enjoy!

From the author Laurelin Paige

Japanese food holds a very special place for my beloved characters Donovan and Sabrina…One of their most memorable dates was a rather private meal that ensured neither of them would ever look at a dumpling again without thinking of each other. Check out Dirty Filthy Rich Men for ideas on how to make this meal more, uh, intimate.

GOOD LUCK DUMPLINGS

FOR *DIRTY FILTHY RICH MEN* BY LAURELIN PAIGE

These pan-fried dumplings are very easy to make! They are filled with ground beef, seasoned with fresh ginger, sesame oil, and fresh scallions. You can serve them with your favorite sauce or prepare the traditional dipping sauce, made from soy sauce and rice vinegar. Whatever you serve them with, you will be in love with this recipe. Just try it!

Prep time: 20 min | Cook time: 15 min | Total time: 35 min

Ingredients

Filling and Wrapping:

400 grams ground beef

6 scallions, thinly sliced

1 teaspoon minced fresh ginger

2 tablespoons toasted sesame oil

1 teaspoon salt, or to taste

25-30 round dumpling wrappers, softened

Pan Frying:

2 tablespoons cooking oil

2 tablespoons water

Dipping Sauce:

3 tablespoons soy sauce

1 tablespoon rice vinegar

Other

sesame seeds

chili flakes

chopped scallions

Instructions

1. To make the filling, in a large bowl, stir together raw beef, ginger, sesame oil, and salt. Mix until well combined and smooth. Add the scallions and mix again.

2. Set aside small dish of water. Scoop about 1 tablespoon of the beef mixture onto single wrapper. Dip finger into water and run it along round edges of wrapper to moisten. Fold wrapper in half and pinch along edges to seal. Use more water if needed. Repeat until beef filling is used up.

3. Drape damp paper towel over assembled dumplings to avoid drying out.

4. Heat oil in nonstick pan over medium heat until hot. Add dumplings to pan in single layer and cook until browned on bottom, about 5 minutes. Pour about 2 tablespoons of water over dumplings and cover with lid until cooked through, about 5 minutes. Work in batches if pan cannot fit all simultaneously.

5. Uncover and transfer cooked dumplings to serving plates. Combine sauce ingredients in dip bowl. Sprinkle with sesame seeds, chili flakes, and scallions. Serve and enjoy!

CHESS-TOPPED VEGETARIAN POTPIE

FOR *THE PAWN* BY SKYE WARREN

Vegetarian potpie with lattice top is comfort food like no other! This family favorite has a thick and creamy filling loaded with lots of different veggies. On top is a flaky pie crust done in a lattice pattern. This recipe perfectly combines the rich and savory flavors of the cooked vegetables into a pie dish. Just try it and you'll be amazed!

🕐 **Prep time: 1 hr 30 min | Cook time: 40 min | Total: 2 hr 10 min**

Ingredients

Dough

2 cups all-purpose flour

3/4 teaspoon salt

2/3 cup butter, chilled + more buttering the dish

5-6 tablespoons ice-cold water

Filling

1/2 cup butter

1 celery stalk, chopped

1 onion, chopped

3 carrots, chopped

1/2 cup all-purpose flour

1 3/4 cups vegetable stock

1 cup milk

1 teaspoon salt

1/2 teaspoon pepper

1/4 teaspoon dried thyme

1 cup peas

1 cup corn

1 cup broccoli

1 green bell pepper, chopped

1 red bell pepper, chopped

1 egg, lightly beaten

Instructions

1. To make the filling, in a large pan, melt butter over medium heat. Add all vegetables and cook until soft, about 5 to 8 minutes.
2. Sprinkle flour over vegetables and cook for 1 minute, stirring frequently. Stir in the vegetable stock and milk. Cook and stir until mixture is thickened and bubbly.
3. Add salt, pepper, and thyme. Stir, remove from heat and set aside.
4. To make the dough, combine all ingredients in a food processor and blend until a dough forms. Add more water as needed.
5. Separate the dough in half. Lightly flour a working surface. Roll out the first part of dough into a large circle enough to fit in a 9-inch pie pan. Butter the baking dish and transfer rolled dough inside. Roll the other part of the dough and cut into 3/4-inch-wide strips.
6. Place the filling over the pie base. Arrange strips in lattice pattern. Refrigerate for at least 1 hour.
7. Preheat oven to 400 degrees Fahrenheit / 200 degrees Celsius and brush the pie with the egg.
8. Bake for 35 to 40 minutes or until pastry is golden.

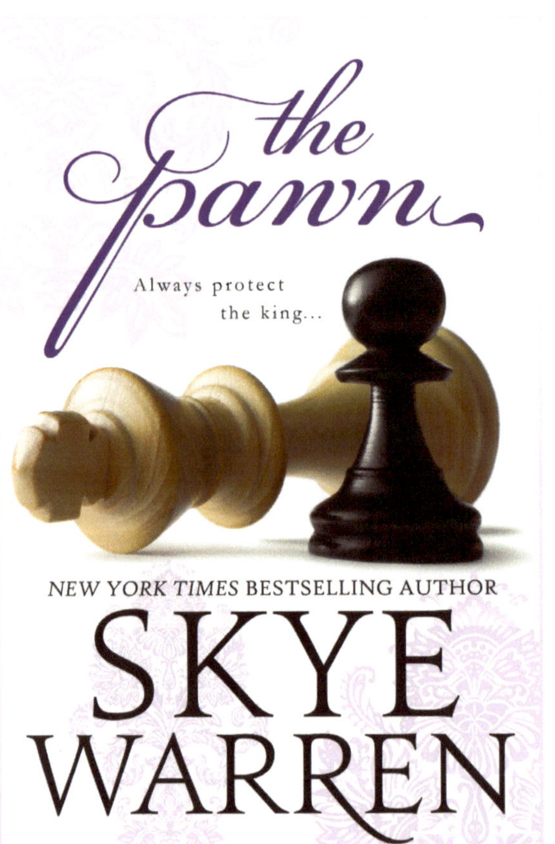

Excerpt from The Pawn by Skye Warren

My eyes widen as I realize this has a second floor, reachable by a spiral staircase. Little angels with trumpets are carved into the mahogany near the top. At the bottom, hands reach out of the flames.

Okay, that's disturbing.

What's even more disturbing is that this room seems made for me. The fire's already burning with a faint, pleasant crackle. There's a gleaming rustic wood chess set lined up in the center of the table.

On the table beside the fireplace is a stack of books—Fairy Tales from around the Mediterranean, The Myth of Homer Revealed. It's too much to think Gabriel spends his evenings reading Greek mythology. These are for me.

"Ready to play?" comes a low voice.

I whirl, dropping the book I'm holding. Fairy Tales from around the Mediterranean lands spread open, its spine stretched. I pick it up before it bends, hugging the large volume to my chest. "Play?"

He steps out from behind the spiral staircase. Was he waiting for me there? "Chess."

What would you do with her? Damon asked.

Play chess, Gabriel answered, turning me into a joke.

"No, thank you."

"Do you think you can say no?"

Defiance burns in my veins. My mind, my soul. That's my leverage, Candy said, and I don't plan to give him any. "You bought my body, that's all."

"I bought all of you."

"You can make me move around the pieces. Is that what you want?" An empty brainless automaton. That's all I'd give him, as plain as the actual pawn piece on the board. Chess is the game my daddy taught me, the game he played with me every week. And this is the man who ruined him. It would be a betrayal to play it with him.

He eyes the chess set with something like regret. "I'll leave you to your reading, then. I have some work to finish."

"Great," I manage, my voice tight.

I'm a little freaked out by Gabriel's uncanny knowledge of me. Justin got me a tennis bracelet for our last anniversary, shiny and bland. This is officially the sweetest thing anyone has ever done for me. From the man I hate the most.

DESSERTS

SCARLETT'S MOIST BROWNIES

FOR *JOCK ROW* BY SARA NEY

You've never had brownies quite like
these. We can guarantee that!

⏱ **Prep Time: 15 min | Cook Time: 55 min | Inactive Time: 2 hr | Yield: 12 servings**

Ingredients

For the brownies

1 cup cane sugar

½ cup brown sugar

¾ cup all-purpose gluten-free
flour, plus more for dusting

½ teaspoon salt

2/3 cup Dutch cocoa powder

½ cup powdered sugar

2 eggs, room temperature

½ cup canola oil

1 tablespoon water

1 teaspoon vanilla extract

16 ounces milk chocolate bar

For the top of the brownies

¾ cup white chocolate chips

¼ cup dark chocolate chips

Instructions

1. Preheat the oven to 325 degrees Fahrenheit and brush a 9-by-9 baking pan with melted coconut oil (or spray with nonstick spray), then lightly dust with flour.
2. In a medium-size bowl, combine the cane sugar, brown sugar, gluten-free flour, and salt.
3. Then, sift in the cocoa powder and powdered sugar.
4. In a large bowl, use an electric mixer to beat the eggs and canola oil together.
5. Next, add the water and vanilla extract.
6. Slowly add the dry ingredients to the wet ingredients, mixing between to thoroughly combine.
7. Use a knife to roughly chop the chocolate, then fold into the batter using a spatula.
8. Pour the batter into the prepared baking pan and cook for 55 minutes, or until a toothpick comes out clean from the center of the brownies.
9. Remove the brownies, then add the white chocolate and dark chocolate chips.
10. Once melted, use a toothpick or spoon to gently spread over the brownies.
11. Allow the brownies to cool for at least two hours before slicing.

Ingredients

For the crust

20 Oreo cookies

6 graham crackers

¼ cup brown sugar

½ cup butter, melted

For the filling

¾ cup milk

2 cups semisweet chocolate chips

1 teaspoon espresso powder

3 8-ounce packages cream cheese, softened

1 cup pure cane sugar

4 eggs, room temperature

1½ teaspoon vanilla

2 tablespoons all-purpose flour

CHOCOLATE CHEESECAKE

FOR *THE SILVER SWAN* BY AMO JONES

There are few things more decadent than
this rich chocolate cheesecake!

🕐 **Prep Time: 25 min | Cook Time: 75 minutes | Inactive Time: 60 minutes | Yield: 8 servings**

Instructions

For the crust

1. Preheat the oven to 375 degrees Fahrenheit and grease a 9-inch springform pan, then place the pan on a baking sheet.
2. Add the Oreos, graham crackers, sugar, and melted butter to a food processor.
3. Pulse until the cookies are thoroughly crumbled.
4. Then, press the moist crumbs into the bottom of the prepared pan.
5. Bake for 15 minutes, then allow to cool for at least 10 minutes before adding the filling.

For the filling

1. Reduce the heat to 350 degrees Fahrenheit.
2. In a microwave-safe bowl, combine the milk and chocolate.
3. Then, place the bowl in the microwave for one minute before stirring to thoroughly combine the chocolate and milk.
4. Pour that mixture into a large mixing bowl with the espresso powder, softened cream cheeses, and sugar.
5. Use an electric mixer to combine these ingredients for roughly 1-2 minutes.
6. Then add the eggs one at a time, mixing between.
7. Finally, add the vanilla extract and flour to the mixture.
8. After the final two ingredients have been added and mixed in, pour the filling over the cooled crust.
9. Bake for 60 minutes, then turn off the oven and crack the door to allow the cheesecake to cool for one hour.
10. For best results, allow the cheesecake to cool for 30 minutes outside of the oven before refrigerating overnight.
11. Garnish the cheesecake with whipped cream, strawberries, and chocolate syrup.

DIABLO COOKIES

🕐 **Prep time: 15 min | Total time: 40 min**

Ingredients

1 1/2 cups all-purpose flour

1 cup cocoa powder

1 teaspoon baking soda

1/2 teaspoon cayenne pepper, or to taste

1 teaspoon cinnamon

1/2 teaspoon black pepper

1 teaspoon ginger powder

3/4 cup chocolate drops

2 large eggs

1 cup brown sugar

1 cup white sugar plus extra to sprinkle

1/2 cup vegetable oil

1 tablespoon vanilla extract

Instructions

1. Preheat oven to 350 degrees Fahrenheit. Line a baking sheet with parchment paper. Set aside.
2. In a large bowl, sift flour, cocoa powder, baking soda, cayenne pepper, cinnamon, black pepper, and ginger powder. Stir in chocolate chips.
3. In a medium bowl, whisk eggs. Add both sugars, oil, and vanilla. Stir into flour mixture until well combined.
4. Divide the mixture into 13 balls. Flatten cookies slightly. Sprinkle each cookie with sugar. Place cookies in the lined baking sheet with a big distance from each other.
5. Bake for about 15 minutes or until they start to crack. They should still be fudgy in the middle. Leave on the baking sheet until cooled.

PROSECCO GRAPES

FOR *SWAY* BY ADRIANA LOCKE

If you're looking for a new way to enjoy
Prosecco, this is for you!

Prep Time: 10 min | Inactive Time: 12 hr | Yield: 4 servings

Ingredients

- 8 cups green grapes
- 1 bottle Prosecco
- 1 cup cane sugar

Instructions

1. Wash the grapes and add them to a large bowl.
2. Pour the bottle of Prosecco over the grapes, then refrigerate overnight.
3. After they've soaked overnight, drain the grapes.
4. Then, roll the grapes in 1 cup of cane sugar.
5. Place in the freezer for at least one hour, then enjoy!

From the author

Both *Sway* and this recipe will ensure you never look at grapes the same way again!

Excerpt from Sway by Adriana Locke

"Tell me the grapes came out!" Lola giggles through the phone.

"Of course they did," I laugh, "but I'm not telling you how or where."

OREO-STUFFED COOKIES

FOR *THE LOCKER ROOM* BY MEGHAN QUINN

Oreos and chocolate chip cookies?! These stuffed cookies are a must-try dessert!

Prep Time: 30 min | Cook Time: 15 min | Inactive Time: 1 hr | Yield: 15 cookies

Ingredients

3 cups all-purpose flour

2 teaspoons cornstarch

1 teaspoon baking powder

1 teaspoon baking soda

½ teaspoon salt

1 cup unsalted butter, room temperature

½ cup pure cane sugar

1 cup light brown sugar

2 eggs, room temperature

1 ½ teaspoons vanilla extract

¾ cup semisweet chocolate chips, plus more for topping

20 Oreo cookies

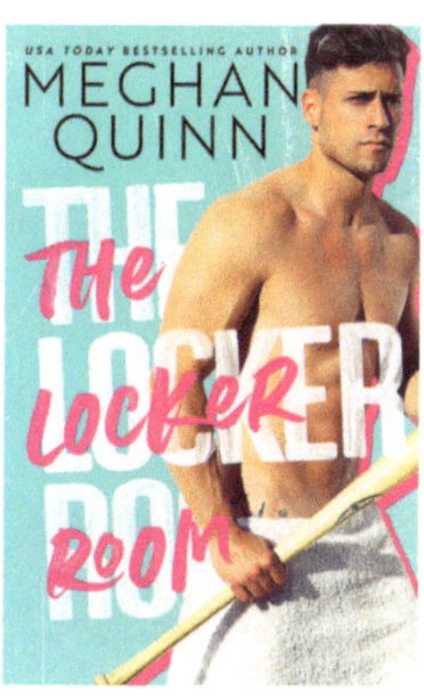

Instructions

1. In a medium mixing bowl, combine the flour, cornstarch, baking powder, baking soda, and salt.
2. In a large bowl, use an electric mixer to combine the butter, cane sugar, and brown sugar.
3. Next, add one egg at a time, mixing between.
4. Then, add the vanilla extract.
5. Slowly add the dry ingredients to the wet ingredients, then fold in the chocolate chips.
6. Crumble 5 Oreo cookies into the cookie batter, then chill the dough in the refrigerator for 30 minutes.
7. After 30 minutes, take one tablespoon of cookie dough and cover the top of an Oreo.
8. Then, take another tablespoon and cover the bottom (the Oreo should be completely covered in dough by the end).
9. Repeat this process with the rest of the dough.
10. Place the prepared Oreos on a baking sheet lined with parchment paper, then chill for 30 minutes in the freezer.
11. Preheat the oven to 375 degrees Fahrenheit, and bake the cookies for 15 minutes.
12. Once you pull the stuffed cookies out of the oven, top with the rest of the chocolate chips.
13. Cool for 10 minutes before enjoying.

CHOCOLATE CHIP COOKIES

FOR *FOR THE LOVE OF ENGLISH* BY A.M. HARGROVE

Few things in life are better than a warm
chocolate chip cookie and glass of milk. This
easy recipe yields the best cookies!

Prep Time: 10 min | Cook Time: 15 Min | Yield: 12 Cookies

Ingredients

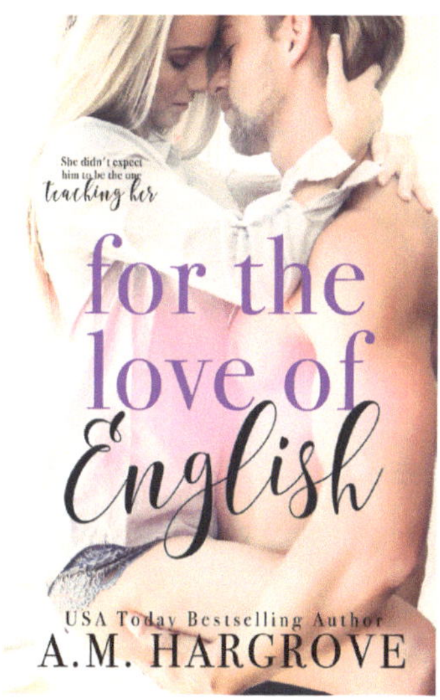

1 cup all-purpose flour

½ teaspoon baking powder

¼ teaspoon salt

½ cup unsalted butter, softened

1/3 cup cane sugar

1/3 cup brown sugar

1 egg

1 teaspoon vanilla extract

1 ½ cups chocolate chips

Instructions

1. Preheat the oven to 375 degrees Fahrenheit and line two baking sheets with parchment paper.
2. Combine the flour, baking soda, and salt in a medium-size bowl.
3. In a large bowl, use an electric mixer to beat together the butter, cane sugar, and brown sugar for 2 minutes.
4. After 2 minutes, add the egg and vanilla extract.
5. Beat again for 1 minute until smooth, then slowly sift in the dry ingredients.
6. Use the mixer to combine the ingredients, then use a spatula to fold in 1 cup of chocolate chips.
7. Then, use a medium-size cookie scoop to place the dough on the prepared baking sheets.
8. Bake the cookies for 12 minutes, then place the rest of the chocolate chips on top of the cookies.
9. Bake for another 2-3 minutes, then remove from the oven.
10. Allow the cookies to cool, then enjoy!

PEPPERMINT STICKS

Ingredients

- 1 cup butter
- 1 1/2 cups confectioners' sugar
- 1 egg
- 1 teaspoon vanilla
- 2 1/2 cups flour
- 1 teaspoon baking soda
- 1 teaspoon cream of tartar

Instructions

1. Beat the first four ingredients together.
2. In a separate bowl, mix the last three ingredients, then add to the butter mixture.
3. Divide the dough in half. To one half, add 1 teaspoon red food color and ¼ teaspoon peppermint extract.
4. Heat the oven to 375 degrees Fahrenheit.
5. Drop dough in alternate pieces (from the two halves) into a greased 9-by-13-inch pan. Pat dough, swirling colors.
6. Bake for 15 minutes. DO NOT OVERBAKE. Even a minute over takes these from perfection to "heh."
7. Cut immediately into sticks and sift additional confectioners' sugar on top.

From the author

Growing up, my mom made these peppermint sticks every year. They're such a family favorite, she's still making them to this day, multiple batches per season! Obviously, this was the first recipe that came to mind to go along with my steamy Christmas rom-com series, Reindeer Falls!

BANOFFEE PIE

FOR *EVERSEA* BY NATASHA BOYD

Banoffee pie is a great English dessert made from bananas, cream, and dulce de leche, combined on buttery crumbled biscuits. This dessert tastes like heaven and it's super easy to make, so you will definitely want to prepare again and again!

Prep time: 25 min | Chill time: 2 hr | Total time: 2 hr 25 min

Ingredients

Crust

1 1/2 cups graham cracker crumbs

6 tablespoons unsalted butter, melted

1 teaspoon vanilla extract

Filling

1 14-ounce can dulce de leche

3 bananas, sliced

1 1/2 cups heavy cream

2 tablespoons powdered sugar

chocolate shavings, swirls, or sprinkles for topping

Instructions

1. Preheat the oven to 350 degrees Fahrenheit. Set the oven rack to the middle position of the oven.
2. In a medium-size bowl, combine graham cracker crumbs, melted butter, and vanilla. Mix to combine.
3. Spread the mixture into a 9-inch pie plate or tart dish. Press the crumbs evenly up the sides and along the bottom of the dish. Bake for 7-8 minutes. Remove the crust from the oven and allow to cool completely.
4. Spread the dulce de leche on the bottom of the crust. Chill for 2 hours.
5. Whip the cream and powdered sugar until stiff peaks form.
6. Place the sliced bananas over the top the toffee. Spread the whipped cream over the top of the banana slices.
7. Sprinkle with chocolate curls and serve! Pie must be stored in the refrigerator. Will keep for 2-3 days.

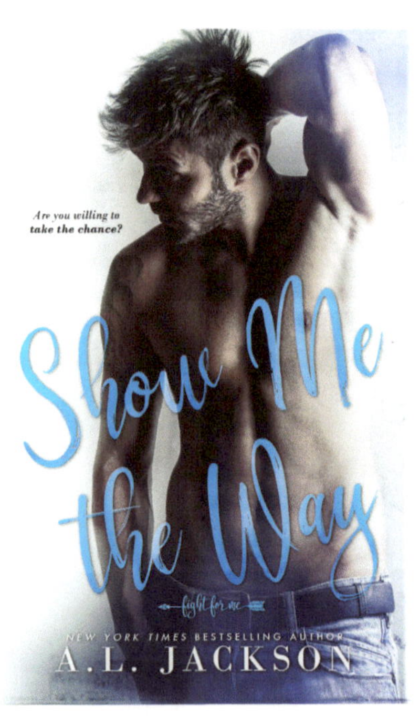

Excerpt from Show Me The Way by A.L. Jackson

I watched her light footsteps as she crossed the floor, the way her hair fell across the silky skin of her neck as she leaned over to pull the piping hot cherry pie from the oven.

A pie that smelled like its own kind of miracle.

"You really are trying to ruin me, aren't you, woman?"

She giggled. Fuck, that was cute, too. "How's that?"

"I think you know exactly what you're doing."

"And what would that be?" Playing along, each of her words dripped with the sexy tease.

"Charming me with those pies and bewitching me with that body."

"If that's all it takes," she said, tossing me a grin as she cut into the pie that had been her grandmother's recipe.

CHERRY PIE

Is there anything better than a classic cherry pie?

⏱ **Prep Time: 30 min | Cook Time: 35 min | Inactive Time: 45 min | Yield: 10 servings**

Ingredients

2 prepared pie crusts

6 cups sweet cherries, pitted

½ cup pure cane sugar

¼ cup corn starch

1 tablespoon lemon juice

1 teaspoon ground cinnamon

1 egg

1 tablespoon milk

1 tablespoon cane sugar

Instructions

1. Preheat the oven to 425 degrees Fahrenheit and grease a 9-inch-wide pie pan.
2. Lay the first pie crust on the inside of the pie pan.
3. In a medium-size bowl, add the cherries, sugar, corn starch, lemon juice, and cinnamon.
4. Allow the mixture to sit for 15 minutes, then drain any liquid and add to the prepared pie pan.
5. Next, take the second pie crust and cut into long strips.
6. Using the strips of pie crust, create a lattice crust over the top by folding one piece of dough over one strip and over the next.
7. Continue this process until the pie is covered, then tuck the excess dough and pinch the edges to seal the pie.
8. Chill the pie for 30 minutes in the refrigerator.
9. In a small bowl, combine the egg, milk, and cane sugar.
10. Brush over the top of the pie, the bake for 35 minutes or until golden brown.
11. Cool for 15 minutes before enjoying with your favorite ice cream!

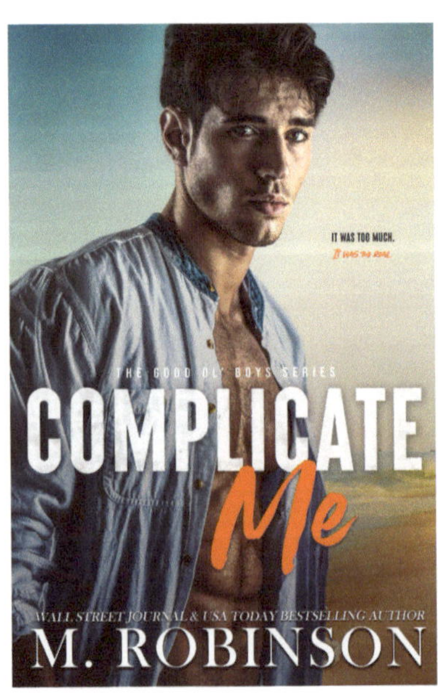
IT WAS TOO MUCH.
It was too real.
THE GOOD OL' BOYS SERIES
COMPLICATE
Me
WALL STREET JOURNAL & USA TODAY BESTSELLING AUTHOR
M. ROBINSON

LEMON TARTS

FOR *COMPLICATE ME* BY M. ROBINSON

These delicious lemon tarts have a buttery crispy crust and silky fresh filling. It's a pleasure to prepare this dessert at home. Also your friends and family will be amazed for sure!

Ingredients

Crust

1 ¾ cups all-purpose flour, plus extra for rolling

⅔ cup butter, chilled, plus extra for greasing the tins

⅓ cup powdered sugar

1/2 teaspoon vanilla powder

1 teaspoon soy milk

Filling

3 ½ tablespoons custard powder

3 cups milk

1 lemon, zested

3 drops lemon oil

½ cup cane sugar, or a little more to taste

¾ teaspoon agar powder

pinch of turmeric

Instructions

1. Grease the tart tins with butter. Set aside.
2. Add all the ingredients for the crust to a food processor and pulse until just combined. If your pastry is too soft to be rolled out, place it in an airtight container and chill it in the fridge for about 1 hour.
3. On a lightly floured surface, roll out your pastry to about 5 mm thick. Using a circular cookie cutter slightly larger than your tart tins, cut rounds out from the pastry.
4. Transfer the pastry rounds to your tart tins and press the pastry against the bottom and sides. If there are any holes, patch them up with more pastry. Pierce the bottoms with a fork. Preheat the oven to 180 degrees Celsius/350 degrees Fahrenheit. When the oven is ready, bake the shells for around 15 minutes or until the edges are slightly golden brown. Set aside to cool.
5. To make the filling, in a small bowl, combine the custard powder and a few tablespoons of milk until there are no lumps.
6. Add all the custard ingredients to a medium-size saucepan over medium-high heat. Whisk consistently while the custard heats up. Gently boil the custard for about 3-5 minutes, then remove from the heat.
7. The custard may have little clumps or bubbles throughout. If so, place a sieve over a wide-pouring jug and carefully pour the hot custard in the sieve. The leftover custard should be smooth and free from bubbles.
8. Place all baked tart shells, while they're still in their tins, on a large tray or in a container. Gently pour the custard into each tart shell. Allow them to sit at room temperature for 5 minutes, then transfer them to the fridge for 1-2 hours or until set.
9. The tarts are set if you can insert a toothpick in the middle and the toothpick stands by itself. Then the tarts are ready to serve! Enjoy!

ETON MESS

FOR *MR. MAYFAIR* BY LOUISE BAY

⏱ **Serves: 4-6 | Start to finish: 10 min | Prep: 10 min**

Ingredients

450 grams/1pound berries

(Traditionally, strawberries (my fav) would be used but raspberries, or blueberries, or a mixture works well. Experiment!)

450 ml/2 cups double cream

(Called heavy cream in the US)

5-6 ready-made meringue nests or 2 cups vanilla meringue cookies

(Of course, you can make your own meringue but I'm notoriously horrible at making them because I'm so impatient and they take hours!)

a little sugar

Instructions

1. Take a third of the fruit and blend it up with a little sugar to taste to make a sauce.
2. With the other two thirds of the fruit, hull and chop the strawberries. And chop the other fruit if it's large (don't bother if it's blueberries, for example).
3. In a large bowl, whisk the cream (use an electric whisk if you have one) until you get soft peaks when you pull out the whisk. Don't over whisk! Some people add a little icing sugar to the cream but I don't think it's necessary.
4. Break up three quarters of the meringue into chunks and combine with the cream and two thirds of the chopped fruit. Put into serving dishes.
5. Drizzle the sauce over the servings and top with the rest of the meringue.

From the author

Eton mess dessert is one of my favorite puddings to make AND eat. It's so versatile because it's so delicious. Who doesn't like the combination of meringue, cream, and fruit. It means you can whip it up for a smart dinner party or a casual lunch with your best friend. The best bit? It's super easy to make!

From the author Cora Reilly

When Skye approached me with this amazing project, I knew that I had to contribute a dessert. After all, my book is a sweet mafia romance called Sweet Temptation, so an Italian dessert was a MUST, and my absolute favorite dessert is tiramisu. It's a sinful treat you shouldn't resist... just like my book!

TIRAMISU

FOR *SWEET TEMPTATION* BY CORA REILLY

One of the best things about the tiramisu is that you don't have to bake it. This recipe is special, because it doesn't include raw eggs. It's made with coffee-soaked lady fingers, sweet and creamy mascarpone, and cocoa powder dusted on top. You can make it in only 15 minutes and the result will be fantastic!

Prep time: 15 min | Total time: 15 min

Ingredients

1 1/2 cups heavy whipping cream

250 grams mascarpone cheese, room temperature

1/3 cup granulated sugar

1 teaspoon vanilla extract

1 1/2 cups cold espresso

3 tablespoon coffee-flavored liqueur, optional

1 package lady fingers

cocoa powder for dusting

Instructions

1. In the bowl of a stand mixer, add whipping cream and beat on medium speed. Slowly add sugar and vanilla and continue to beat until stiff peaks.
2. Add mascarpone cheese and mix just until combined. Set aside.
3. In a shallow bowl, add coffee and liqueur. Dip the lady fingers in the coffee mixture and lay them in a single layer on the bottom of an 8-by-8-inch or similar-size pan.
4. Spread half of the mascarpone mixture over the top. Add another layer of dipped lady fingers. Place the remaining mascarpone cream in a piping bag with a large round nozzle, and pipe the cream over the second layer of dipped lady fingers.
5. Dust cocoa powder generously over the top. Refrigerate for at least 5 hours or overnight before serving. Enjoy!

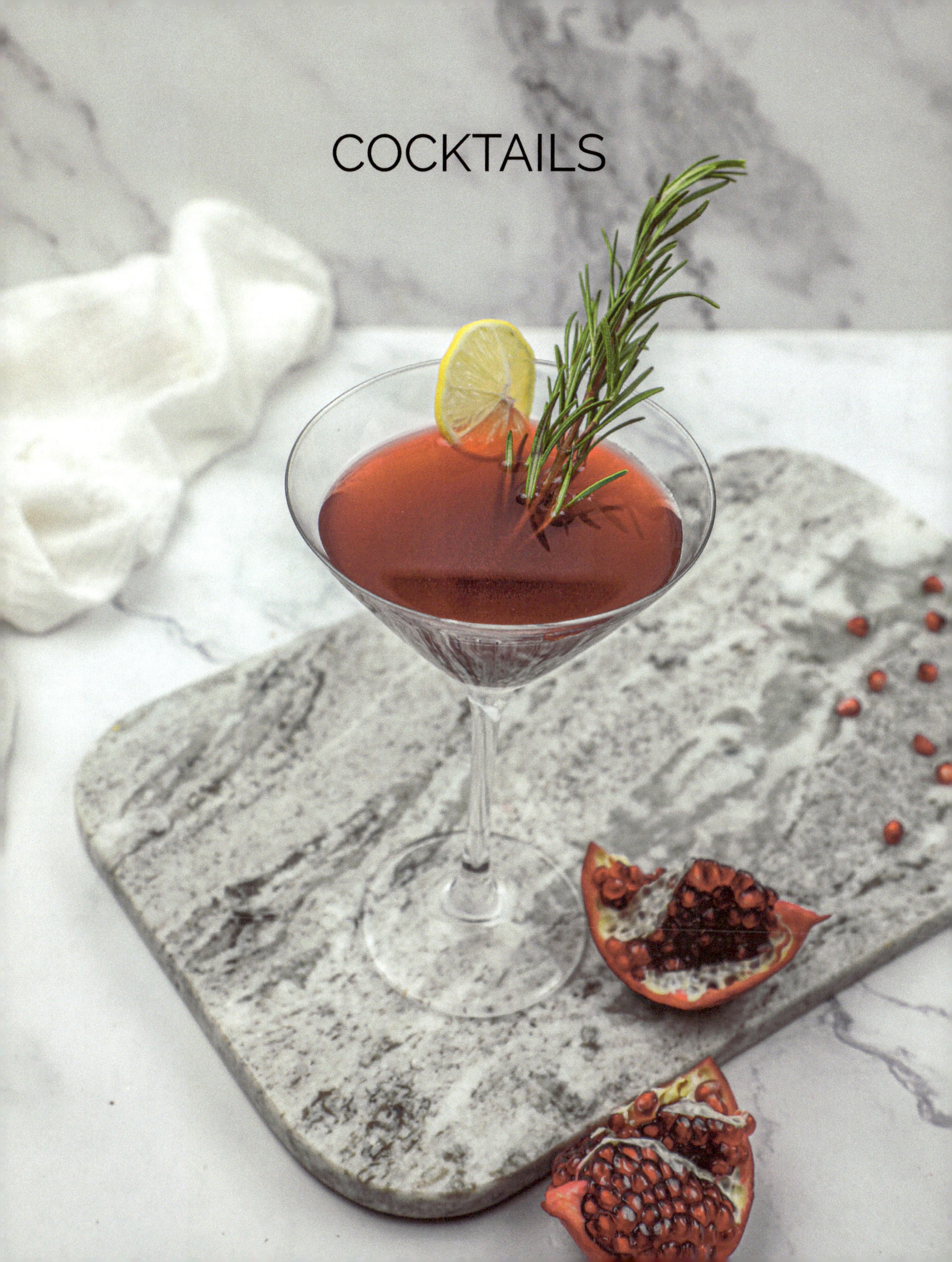
COCKTAILS

UNDERWORLD COCKTAIL

FOR *DESPERATE MEASURES* BY KATEE ROBERT

Looking to experiment with a new cocktail? Test
out the Underworld Cocktail. One sip of this
sultry cocktail will leave you wanting more.

Prep Time: 10 min | Cook Time: 0 min | Yield: 2 servings

Ingredients

4 ounces vodka, chilled

2 ounces blue curaçao liqueur

3 ounces blackberry liqueur

¼ cup cane sugar

2 drops red food coloring

blackberries for garnish

cherries for garnish

ice, optional

Instructions

1. Combine the cane sugar and red food coloring in a bowl.
2. Stir until the sugar is a red/orange color, then pour onto a plate.
3. Take your martini glasses and run a sliced lime along the edges.
4. Turn the glass upside down and place on the plate with the red sugar.
5. Stir until the rim is lined with the sugar, and repeat with the next glass.
6. Pour the chilled vodka, blue curaçao liqueur, and blackberry liqueur into a shaker.
7. Shake for 1-2 minutes, then pour into two martini glasses.
8. Place a pitted cherry or blackberry on a toothpick, then add to your martini.

From the author Katee Robert

The Devil is Jafar's voice in my ear, full of sin and promised pleasure. It might cost me my soul, but what is a soul in comparison with a night's pleasure?

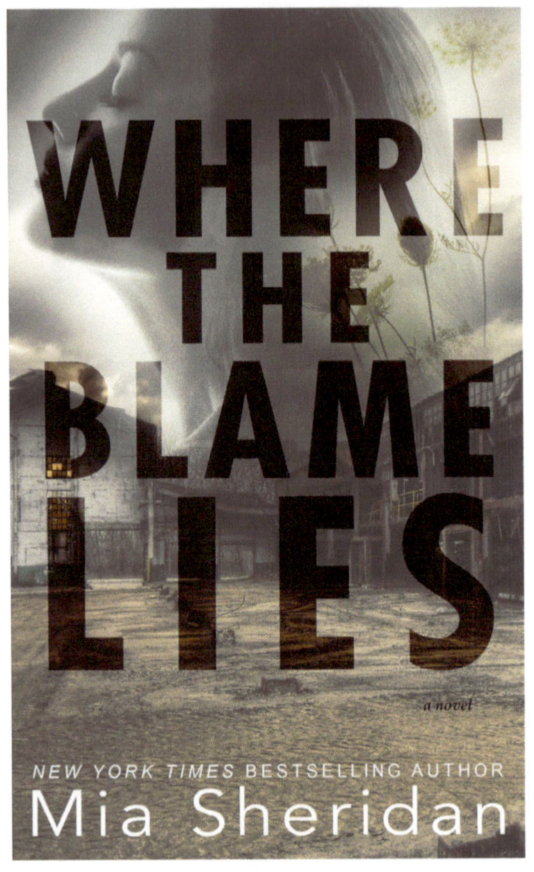

Excerpt from Where the Blame Lies by Mia Sheridan

He laughed, his white teeth flashing, and her stomach gave a little twist. God, he really was distractingly handsome, and as she stood there watching him remove two plates from her cabinet and begin dishing up pizza slices, a tiny sensation of … amazement sparkled through her. In a way, her reaction to the detective was a revelation. She could still respond physically to a man. Whether she'd ever want to take a next step was beside the point. She wasn't broken beyond repair. At least she didn't think so, not after this.

She would not fall into old bad habits— seeking the attention of men in order to validate herself, looking for love in all the wrong places. She would not. Especially when a relationship of any sort with the man tasked with protecting her safety would probably be a conflict of interest. She'd gone down that particular road before and it hadn't ended well. And anyway, it wasn't as if he'd look at her that way, knowing what he knew. But, never mind all that. To realize she could still feel that rush of sexual attraction when she never thought she'd be capable of it again made her feel … hopeful. Happy. As though she'd won something back.

"You're smiling," he noted.

Josie glanced up at Zach in surprise as she brought her fingers to her mouth, smoothing out the smile she hadn't realized she was wearing.

Zach laughed, his eyes dancing. "I meant it as a positive. You should do it more." His smile grew, making him look even more handsome than she'd thought him before. She let out a small laugh as he set the plates down at the table and moved the box to the counter.

Drinks. They'd need drinks. "I, ah, don't have any soda," she said, flustered, moving toward her refrigerator. "But I still have iced tea and water."

"Iced tea would be great," he said, sitting down. As she poured tea in two glasses, she thought about how she'd done the same thing for this man just two days before, and yet that felt like a lifetime ago.

ICED TEA

FOR *WHERE THE BLAME LIES* BY MIA SHERIDAN

There's nothing quite as refreshing as iced tea on a hot day!

⏱ Prep Time: 10 min | Cook Time: 20 min | Inactive Time: 60 min | Yield: 10 servings

Ingredients

8 cups water

6 black tea bags

¼ cup sugar

1 lemon, sliced

10 fresh mint leaves

Instructions

1. Bring four cups of water to a boil, then remove from heat.
2. Add the tea bags and allow them to steep for 15 minutes.
3. Remove the tea bags and mix in the cane sugar.
4. Add the rest of the water, then refrigerate for one hour.
5. Finally, serve over ice and garnish with lemon slices and fresh mint.

MAINE BLUEBERRY MOJITOS

FOR *PRIVATE PROPERTY* BY SKYE WARREN

If you're looking for a refreshing cocktail,
we have the perfect sip for you!

🕐 **Prep Time: 10 min | Cook Time: 15 min | Yield: 3 servings**

Ingredients

For the mint simple syrup

½ cup cane sugar

1 cup water

10 mint leaves

For the mojito (per glass)

2 lime slices

5 mint leaves

2 tablespoons blueberries
(roughly 7-10 blueberries)

ice

1ounce mint simple syrup

2 ounces white rum

2-4 ounces club soda

fresh mint, for garnish

blueberries, for garnish

Instructions

For the mint simple syrup

1. Add the sugar and water to a small saucepan, then bring to a boil.
2. Once all of the sugar is dissolved, remove from heat and add the mint leaves.
3. Steep the leaves for at least 10 minutes.
4. Remove the leaves, then refrigerate.

For the mojito (per glass)

1. Add the lime slices, mint leaves, and blueberries to a glass.
2. Use a muddler to muddle the ingredients to release the flavor.
3. Add the ice, simple syrup, and white rum to the glass, then stir.
4. Finish with club soda, then garnish with fresh mint.

THE PENNY COCKTAIL

FOR *MASTER OF SIN* BY SIENNA SNOW

If you like whiskey AND tequila, this cocktail is for you!

Prep Time: 10 min | Cook Time: 0 Min | Yield: 2 highball drinks (or 4 cocktails)

Ingredients

6 ounces silver tequila

4 ounces Scotch whiskey

2 ounces elderflower liqueur

2 ounces lime juice

1 ounce simple syrup

ice

lime wedges

Instructions

1. Combine all of the ingredients in a cocktail shaker.
2. Shake, strain, and pour over ice.
3. Garnish with lime wedges and enjoy.

From the author

The Penny Cocktail takes the heroine of Master of Sin, Penny Kipos's love of elderflower-infused whiskey and blends it with Sienna Snow's love of tequila into a refreshing and potent cocktail to enjoy any time of the day.

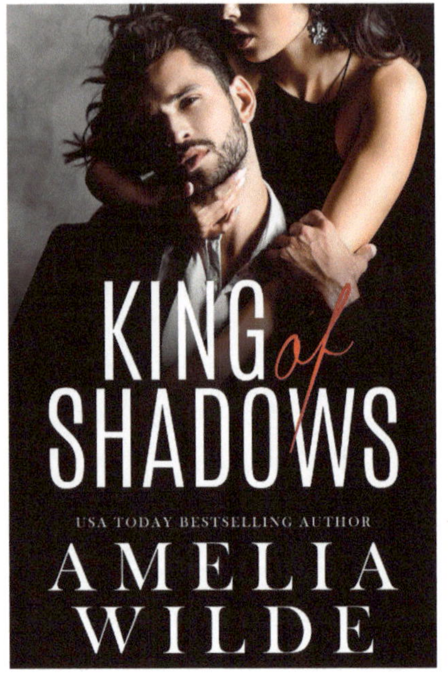

Excerpt from King of Shadows by Amelia Wilde

She tastes sweet and clean and soft, and the panicked little noises at the back of her throat drive me wild, wilder, until there's not much man left at all. Do I pull her into my arms, or does she climb up, her legs wrapped around my waist? Does she cry before I yank her head back by the hair and lick up the length of her neck, or is it after? I bite down on her bottom lip until the moment she starts to scream, and then I pull back. "You didn't eat your dinner."

Persephone is the picture of confusion. "I wasn't hungry."

"Liar." It's nothing to carry her back out to the bedroom, put her on her feet, and bend her over the tray. "You're starving. You just don't know it."

"I was reading." Her voice shakes. "I meant to come finish it."

"When I tell you to finish something, you do it first or you'll suffer the consequences."

A shiver rocks her under my hand, electric, and she murmurs something into the pomegranate.

"I can't hear you."

"Please."

Her voice is a bolt through the room, and that's all it takes. I thought I was undone before. That was nothing compared to now. I force her down onto her knees and reduce her clothing to shreds. Indiscriminate. I want her skin exposed to me now. Her perfect pink nipples are already peaked, her thighs spread—she wants this. Fuck me. She wants it as much as she hates it.

The pomegranate next.

I rip it apart, the two halves glistening in my palms, and drop most of it back to the table. Persephone's chest heaves with every breath. She has perfect little tits, a lovely shape, and they'll be even lovelier covered in the juice from the pomegranate. It comes apart easily in my hands.

She doesn't struggle when I take her chin in my hand and tip her head back. She looks up at me with her huge, depthless gaze, lips slightly parted. I work a thumb between her teeth and force them open farther.

"Eat."

POMEGRANATE MARTINI

When you really need a colorful cocktail that is perfect for parties, you need this pomegranate martini. It is beautiful and super easy to make. The orange and pomegranate are a great combination that you'll love for sure!

🕐 **Total time: 5 min**

Ingredients

1 1/2 ounce (45 ml) vodka

1ounce (30 ml) pomegranate liqueur

1/5 ounce (15 ml) lemon juice, freshly squeezed

3/4 ounce (25 ml) orange juice, freshly squeezed

3/4 ounce (25 ml) triple sec

1/2 ounce (15 ml) pomegranate juice

1 teaspoon pomegranate seeds

lemon slice for serving

rosemary sprig for serving

Instructions

1. Pour all ingredients into a cocktail shaker with ice.
2. Shake for 25 seconds and serve in a chilled martini glass.
3. Garnish with lemon slice and rosemary sprig. Add pomegranate seeds and serve.

WEDDING TOAST FRENCH 75

FOR *THE RELUCTANT BRIDE* BY MONICA MURPHY

This French 75 recipe is the perfect cocktail to surprise party guests without a lot of effort. Made with champagne, gin, and simple syrup, this is the perfect drink to make for a celebration or just for fun.

🕐 **Total time: 5 min**

Ingredients

2 ounces (60 ml) gin

¾ ounce (20 ml) lemon juice

½ ounce (15 ml) simple syrup

2 ounces (60 ml) champagne

Instructions

1. Mix the gin, lemon juice, and simple syrup together in a cocktail shaker with ice until very cold.
2. Top with champagne. Serve with lemon peel.

From the author

If you're looking for an elegant yet simple cocktail, the French 75 champagne cocktail is the perfect choice! It also reminds me of the many champagne-soaked moments in my book The Reluctant Bride...

BAKERY & BREAKFAST

BLUEBERRY LEMON THYME SCONES

FOR *DRIVE ME WILD* BY MELANIE HARLOW

Ingredients

3 3/4 cups all-purpose flour

2 teaspoons salt

2 tablespoons baking powder

1/2 cup sugar

1 teaspoon lemon zest

1 pint blueberries

2 1/2 cups cold heavy cream

Glaze

1 teaspoon fresh thyme leaves

1 cup powdered sugar

4 tablespoons lemon juice

1 teaspoon lemon zest

Instructions

1. Preheat oven to 375 degrees Fahrenheit.
2. Mix together the flour, salt, baking powder, lemon zest, and sugar.
3. Add the blueberries and incorporate into dry ingredients so they are evenly distributed. Add the heavy cream and mix just until it comes together in the bowl.
4. Turn dough over on table and fold a few times.
   Baker's Note: "I like to knead until the blueberries start to break up, resulting in a nice jammy scone."
5. Shape into a ball and pat down to form a 10-inch circle. Cut into 8 slices and place on parchment sheet. Make sure the scones have at least ½ inch separation between them. Bake at 375 degrees Fahrenheit for about 20 minutes.
   Glaze: Mix all ingredients together and spread on scones once they have cooled.

Excerpt from Drive Me Wilde by Melanie Harlow

"So what's in these things anyway?"

"They're blueberry-lemon-thyme," Blair said. "I call it a BLT." She grinned triumphantly. "Try one. I made plenty."

"I can't. My hands are filthy."

"Here." She picked one up and held it to my lips. I took a bite, conscious of the way everyone in the room was watching us.

But as I tasted her creation, I had to admit I understood why widowed old Charlie Frankel might be back every morning. "Wow. It is good. I thought it would be sweet like a donut."

She shook her head and smiled proudly. "My favorite things are both sweet and savory. I love the way the thyme and lemon balance the sugar and fruit. Here, have another bite."

IRISH SODA BREAD

Homemade bread has never been so easy to make!

Prep Time: 10 min | Cook Time: 45 min | Yield: 10 servings

Ingredients

1 ¾ cups buttermilk

1 egg, room temperature

4 ½ cups all-purpose flour

3 tablespoons pure cane sugar

1 teaspoon baking soda

1 teaspoon salt

5 tablespoons unsalted butter, cubed

½ cup raisins

Instructions

1. Preheat the oven to 400 degrees Fahrenheit and line a Dutch oven with parchment paper.
2. In a small bowl, whisk the buttermilk and egg together.
3. In another bowl, add the flour, cane sugar, baking soda, and salt.
4. Add the cubed butter to the flour mixture, then use your fingers to combine the butter and flour mixture until the butter resembles pea-size crumbs.
5. Next, pour in the buttermilk mixture and add the raisins.
6. Use your hands to gently fold the dough and knead until the dough can be formed into a ball.
7. Place the dough int the prepared Dutch oven, and bake for 45 minutes.
8. Allow the bread to cool for 15 minutes before slicing and serving.

From the author

This bread is perfect for beginner bakers. With raisins or without, it comes together easily and in no time you are ready to enjoy delicious bread. All you need to do is find a roaring fire, a mysterious and sexy Irishman and enjoy!

WAFFLES

FOR *VOYEUR* BY FIONA COLE

Waffles are one of those breakfasts that can instantly transport you back to childhood. With fresh berries and delicious maple syrup, THIS is the breakfast of champions.

Prep Time: 10 min | Cook Time: 20 min | Yield: 5 servings

Ingredients

1 ½ cups all-purpose flour

2 tablespoons cane sugar

2 teaspoons baking powder

¼ teaspoon salt

¾ cup milk

2 eggs, room temperature

4 tablespoons unsalted butter, melted

2 teaspoons vanilla extract

maple syrup

fresh berries

Instructions

1. In a large bowl, combine the flour, sugar, baking powder, salt, milk, eggs, melted butter, and vanilla extract.
2. Whisk for 1-2 minutes until smooth.
3. Spray nonstick spray on a waffle iron, then add 2 tablespoons of batter to the waffle iron.
4. Press down on the waffle iron and allow to cook for about 2 minutes.
5. Then, use a spatula to remove the waffle from the iron and place on a plate to the side.
6. Repeat this process with the rest of the batter.
7. When all the waffles are cooked, serve with maple syrup and fresh berries.

HARD
PRESSED

Note from the characters

Dear Jackson, I'm not sure why, but I couldn't get buns out of my mind today, so I whipped some up. That seemed like the appropriate baked good for getting naked in your living room. Please burn this note after you read it. Annette

CINNAMON ROLLS

FOR *HARD PRESSED* BY KATE CANTERBARY

In Sweden and Finland, cinnamon rolls are traditionally enjoyed during a coffee break. Those countries even have a national cinnamon bun day, which is on October 4. The best news is that we don't need a special day to celebrate these fragrant and fluffy buns! Just gather all ingredients and turn on the heat!

Prep time: 2 hr | Cook time: 20 min | Total time: 2 hr 20 min

Ingredients

Dough

3/4 cup warm milk

2 1/4 teaspoons quick rise yeast

1/4 cup granulated sugar

1 large egg, at room temperature

1 egg yolk

1/4 cup unsalted butter, melted

3 cups all-purpose flour, plus more for dusting

3/4 teaspoon salt

Filling

2/3 cup brown sugar

1 1/2 tablespoons cinnamon

1/4 cup unsalted butter, softened

Frosting

120 grams cream cheese, softened

3 tablespoons unsalted butter, softened

1/4 cup powdered sugar

1 teaspoon vanilla extract

Instructions

1. Place the warm milk in a bowl of an electric mixer and sprinkle yeast on top. Add in sugar, egg, egg yolk, and melted butter. Mix until well combined. Using a wooden spoon, stir in the flour and salt, until a dough begins to form.
2. Place dough hook on stand mixer and knead dough on medium speed for 6-8 minutes. Dough should form into a nice ball and be slightly sticky. If it's too sticky, add in 2 tablespoons flour.
3. Transfer dough ball to a well-oiled bowl, cover with plastic wrap and a warm towel. Allow dough to rise for 1 hour, or until doubled in size.
4. Transfer dough to a well-floured surface and roll out into a 14-by-9-inch rectangle. Spread softened butter over dough, leaving a ¼-inch margin at the far side of the dough.

5. In a small bowl, mix together brown sugar and cinnamon. Use your hands to sprinkle mixture over the buttered dough. Tightly roll dough up, starting from the 9-inch side and place seam side down, making sure to seal the edges of the dough as best you can.

6. Cut into about 1-inch sections. Place cinnamon rolls in a greased suitable baking pan. Cover with plastic wrap and a warm towel and let rise again for 30-45 minutes.

7. Preheat oven to 350 degrees Fahrenheit. Remove plastic wrap and towel and bake cinnamon rolls for 20-25 minutes or until just slightly golden brown on the edges. Allow them to cool for 5-10 minutes before frosting.

8. To make the frosting, in the bowl of an electric mixer, combine cream cheese, butter, powdered sugar, and vanilla extract. Beat until smooth and fluffy. Pour over cinnamon rolls and serve immediately. Enjoy!

HILL FAMILY PANCAKES

FOR *NET WORTH* BY AMELIA WILDE

What better way to start the day than with pancakes?

🕐 **Prep Time: 10 min | Cook Time: 20 min | Yield: 5 servings**

Ingredients

1 cup Bisquick

2 tablespoons cane sugar

1/4 teaspoon baking powder

¼ teaspoon baking soda

1 cup milk

1 egg

2 tablespoons butter, melted

1 teaspoon vanilla extract

maple syrup

Instructions

1. In a large bowl, whip egg whites until they have soft peaks.
2. Add sugar and vanilla to whipped egg whites.
3. Fold in milk.
4. In another bowl, combine Bisquick, baking powder, and baking soda. Add to egg white mixture.
5. In separate bowl, combine egg yolks and melted butter. Add to batter.
6. Add food coloring to match the occasion if desired.
7. Whisk for no more than 2 minutes.
8. Let sit for 15 minutes (10 in a pinch).
9. Spray nonstick spray on a pan or griddle, and turn on the heat to medium.
10. Then pour 2 tablespoons of the batter onto the hot pan.
11. When bubbles pop and remain holes on top of pancake, flip the pancake onto the other side.
12. Cook for about 30-60 seconds, then use a spatula to set on a plate.
13. Repeat steps 9–11 for rest of batter.
14. Finally, pour maple syrup over your pancake stack and enjoy!

net worth

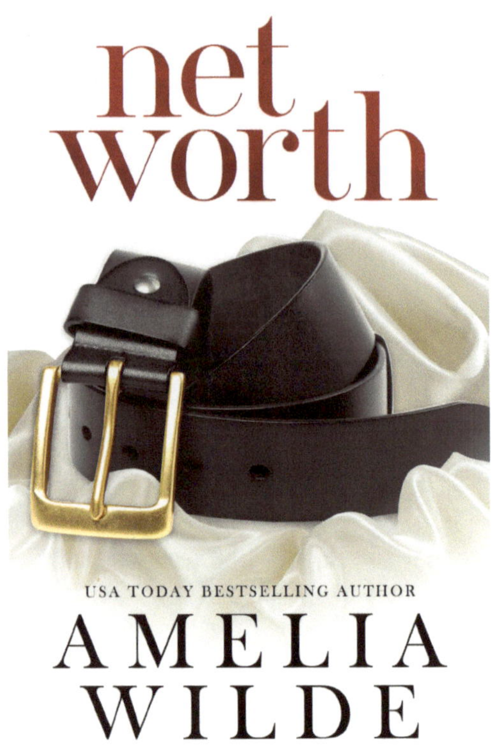

From the author

When Mason Hill's family was still a happy one, his dad took great pleasure in making pancakes on Saturday. James Hill's famous recipe is more elaborate than most, but that's only because he wanted his wife and kids to have the best.

Excerpt from Net Worth by Amelia Wilde

Jameson drops his fork onto his plate with a loud clang of silver hitting china. "A pleasure as always. I'm so glad we had this little brunch. The table is yours."

"Sit down, fucker."

"No."

I'm out of my seat before he can get around the table, my glass going over in the process, a plate hitting the floor. I catch Jameson with one fist in his shirt, my knee aching, and use all my body weight to put him up against one of the windows. "I can't fix it if you won't tell me what the hell is wrong."

Jameson glowers at me.

Then he throws a punch.

I deflect it in time to stop him from hitting my temple and return both hands to the task in front of me. Another punch. This one is harder to stop. I throw one on instinct and get Jameson across the cheek.

"I can't believe you outsourced the pancakes." The hint of a crooked grin, but I don't buy it. "Dad's special pancakes that he made for us. His own recipe. And you just hand it off to a chef, like what? Like it's a goddamn task on your to-do list?"

"I thought you liked them," I say, but there's a sick feeling in my stomach. Somewhere in between building Phoenix Enterprises and seeking revenge, I've lost my hold on the family. The brunch was supposed to fix that. Instead it's made it worse.

"What's next? You have your secretary buy us Christmas presents? You pay actors to sit around at Thanksgiving pretending to be Mom and Dad? Jesus Christ, Mason." Jameson punches me toward the back of my jaw, and now I'm going to kill him. Now's the day I stop being Jameson's older brother and safety net, I stop worrying about him, I stop noticing the hurt in his eyes. "Remy's not even here. If we can't all be here, just cancel it."

"That's the entire point. We're here because we can't all be together. We can never be together again. This is all there is."

BLACK BEAN BREAKFAST TACOS

These black bean tacos are the perfect breakfast! They are extremely easy to make and it only takes a few minutes to be prepared. The protein in the black beans will satisfy your hunger and will keep your energy high until the next meal.

🕐 **Prep time: 5 min | Cook time: 5 min | Total time: 10 min**

Ingredients

2 small tortillas

1 teaspoon olive oil

1 clove garlic, minced

1 cup fresh corn kernels

1/2 cup canned black beans, rinsed and drained

2 tablespoon fresh chopped parsley leaves + extra to serve

1 pinch paprika

2 large eggs, beaten

salt and pepper to taste

hot sauce, optional

Instructions

1. In a large, nonstick skillet over high heat, warm tortillas, about 1 minute per side. Set aside.
2. Return skillet to medium heat and add olive oil. Add garlic and cook just until fragrant, about 30 seconds.
3. Add corn, black beans, parsley, and paprika. Season with salt and pepper and cook, stirring, until just heated through, about 1 minute.
4. Add eggs and cook, stirring constantly, until just set, about 1-2 minutes more.
5. Spoon egg mixture over tortillas and sprinkle with extra parsley. Serve with hot sauce, if desired.

Excerpt from Survival of the Richest by Skye Warren

Christopher studies the painting through his sunglasses. "Cleopatra?"

There's a hardness to his jaw like it pains him to speak, and as much as I've fought him, I can spare him that. This painting won't be enough to save the library. Nothing will.

"She knows what's coming," I say, softly so no one else hears.

He huffs a laugh. "As it turns out, Sutton was right. You do have the skills of diplomacy we need. You can convince people to do anything. Unfortunately you convinced them to hate us."

I look away and manage a small smile. "And it turns out you were right. It doesn't matter whether they hate you. You have the deed and a wrecking ball."

"It didn't have to be like this," Christopher says, his jaw tight. There's a muscle that works. A slight flare of his nostrils. The slightest signs that he's upset. He had those same signs the day the will was signed, but he would not be swayed then. Not now, either.

Strange, the way I can admire his resolve even as it tears us apart. "It was always like this."

"You can probably make them riot," he remarks, his voice even. "An angry mob."

"To break the windows in? To steal the books? A little counter to the purpose." Besides, the breakfast tacos were too delicious. No one could be in a rage after eating breakfast tacos.

"Or they could form a human chain around the building. It would delay construction, if nothing else."

"And cost you money," I say, gentle now. "If nothing else."

"There's that."

"I'm not going to do that. I made my point."

"Which is what?" He looks genuinely lost. It isn't part of advanced economics theory, what's happening in the streets tonight. It's community. History. These are things he doesn't understand.

"The protest isn't to stop you. It isn't even about you, not really. Protests are a voice for people who have been told not to be quiet. It's the only way we can speak."

From the author

DIAMOND IN THE ROUGH is a dark romance that starts when a woman flies to France. She's looking for her sister, who's gone missing. Holly Frank is determined to find her. Except she finds herself in trouble as soon as she lands. Kidnapped. Thrown into a prison cell. How will she save her sister? Who will save her?

CHOCOLATE AND RASPBERRY CREPES

FOR *DIAMOND IN THE ROUGH* BY SKYE WARREN

If you are a chocolate lover and you also love fresh berries, these crepes will satisfy your cravings. You can serve them for breakfast or enjoy them like a dessert. Gather family and friends and serve these rich chocolate and raspberry crepes. Your guests will thank you!

Prep time: 5 min | Cook time: 20 min | Total time: 25 min

Ingredients

3 eggs

1 cup all-purpose flour

2 tablespoons sugar

2 tablespoons unsweetened cocoa powder

1 1/4 cups buttermilk or sour milk

2 tablespoon melted butter + more for cooking

chocolate spread for serving

1 cup raspberries for serving

1 teaspoon powdered sugar for dusting

Instructions

1. Add all ingredients for the crepes to a blender and blend until smooth.
2. Melt a small piece of butter in a 10-inch nonstick frying pan, over medium-low heat. Pour about 1/4 cup batter into pan and rotate until the batter coats the entire bottom of the pan.
3. Cook until the color of the crepe turns slightly darker. The "wetness" of the batter disappears, which indicates that it's time to flip the crepe.
4. Use a silicone spatula to loosen around the edges of the crepe. Flip it over and cook briefly on the other side. Remove from pan to cool. Do this with the whole batter.
5. Spread some chocolate into each crepe and dust with powdered sugar. Serve with fresh raspberries.

VANILLA CREAM BEIGNETS

FOR *DEVIL'S DEAL* BY ALEATHA ROMIG

This is a dessert that you should drink your coffee with! Invite friends and gather the family and you will see that these vanilla cream beignets disappear in seconds. Everyone will want the recipe because this is the best recipe for beignets!

Serves: 25 | Start to finish: 50 min | Prep: 20 min | Cook: 30 min

Ingredients

Shells:

5 cups vegetable oil, for frying

1 cup milk

1 large egg

2 cups all-purpose flour

2 tablespoons sugar

4 1/2 teaspoons baking powder

1/2 teaspoon salt

1/4 cup unsalted butter, melted

Cream:, Filling:

1 cup whole milk

½ cup heavy cream

4 large egg yolks

½ cup granulated sugar

3½ tablespoons cornstarch

2 teaspoons vanilla extract

1 tablespoon unsalted butter

Instructions

1. To make the cream, in a mixing bowl, whisk together 1/2 cup milk, egg yolks, 1/4 cup sugar, and cornstarch. Set aside.
2. In a medium saucepan, add remaining milk, cream, and sugar. Bring the mixture to a light simmer.
3. Whisk 1/3 cup of the hot liquid into the yolk mixture and continue to mix to prevent yolks from scrambling.
4. Pour yolk mixture into the pan with the remaining hot liquid and whisk together over medium-low heat. Continue to cook the pastry cream to allow the mixture to thicken.
5. Once the mixture is thick enough to coat the back of a spoon, stir in the vanilla and butter and whisk until fully incorporated.

6. Strain mixture into a bowl sitting over an ice bath and allow to cool completely.

7. Cover the cooled pastry cream and place it in the refrigerator for at least an hour or until ready to use.

8. To make the shells, add the vegetable oil to a large, heavy-bottomed pot. (There should be at least 2 inches of oil in the pot and at least 2 inches between the top of the oil and the top of the pot.) Attach the deep-fry thermometer to the pot and begin heating the oil over medium heat to 350 degrees Fahrenheit. Line a baking sheet with paper towels.

9. In a small bowl, whisk together the milk and the egg.

10. In a separate medium bowl, whisk together the flour, sugar, baking powder, and salt. Stir the milk-egg mixture into the dry ingredients, then stir in the melted butter, mixing until a soft dough forms.

11. Once the oil has reached 350 degrees Fahrenheit, use a small ice cream scoop to drop about 1 tablespoon scoops of dough into the oil, careful not to overcrowd the pan.

12. Fry the beignets, flipping them in the oil, for about 2 minutes or until they're golden brown. Using a slotted spoon, transfer the beignets to the paper towel-lined baking sheet.

13. Allow the beignets to cool. Once they are cooled enough to handle, gently insert the pastry filling tip into the doughnut and squeeze the vanilla cream inside. Repeat with all beignets. Sprinkle with powdered sugar. Enjoy!

From the author

Find yourself in the heart of New Orleans. Feel the steam and taste the decadent richness with this favorite delicacy of the ruler of the city, the devil himself, Rett Ramses.